Fireflies at Nightfall

Robin Cannon

Goose River Press
Waldoboro, Maine

Library of Congress Card Number: 2016955767

ISBN: 978-1-59713-172-8

First Printing, 2017

Cover photo by Ruslan Huzau.

Published by
Goose River Press
3400 Friendship Road
Waldoboro ME 04572
e-mail: gooseriverpress@roadrunner.com
www.gooseriverpress.com

Dedication

In Loving Memory of Mocka and Papa

Two Hearts Together Bound Through All Eternity

Acknowledgements

I would like to thank my husband Bob and my three beautiful children Haley, Molly and Colin for their unending patience, love and support. I would especially like to thank my husband Bob for his editorial contributions and my daughter Molly for her skillful photo design of the author.

I would also like to thank John Valeri of *Hartford Books Examiner* for taking the time to read my manuscript and thoughtfully review its contents. In addition, his editing suggestions were invaluable.

Finally, I would like to thank my grandparents, Mary and Ralph, who are no longer with us, but were never far from my mind during the writing of this book. My memory of the special love they shared together inspired the characters of Tilly and Skeet in their later years, and it is to them that I lovingly dedicate this book.

Grow old along with me!
The best is yet to be.

—Robert Browning, *Rabbi Ben Ezra*

Chapter 1

Let Me Out!

Whatever our souls are made of, his and mine are the same.

— Emily Bronte, *Wuthering Heights!*

Trapped. Trapped in my own body...my own head. Can't get out. Think, Tilly, think. What to do? Breathe deeper. Form the words on my tongue and get them to come...out. I can't get them to come...out. Look at Skeet. He still has that reassuring expression after all these years. He is leaning over me now, slipping my long, translucent fingers that had once performed surgery into his gnarled but gentle grip. Oh that mischievous, boyish smile that I have loved...so engaging, so thoroughly unchanged by his storied life. So...so...so...

"Tilly? Fig, darling, are you awake?" he inquires through a whisper in my ear.

His voice is quivering and scratchy as he lovingly bends over me, always the protector. His face has gone unshaven for a few days and he is far too thin. Those rumpled clothes need a good washing and ironing. His eyes are pooled with tears. We are both trapped...trapped by the passage of time.

"Mr. LeMay?" the floor nurse addresses him as she rolls her cart of pills, syrups, and needles into my room. "Mr. LeMay? May I get you something? Would you like some orange juice? You know, you should really go home and get

1

some rest."

"I'm sorry...what?" comes the faint, distracted answer. "Oh...no thank you. I'll just sit here a while longer with my wife."

My husband is gazing into my panicked eyes with loving concern.

"Talk to her, Mr. LeMay," urges the kindly nurse. "It's important that you talk to her. She will hear everything you say."

I do! I do!

"Will she regain her movement...her speech?" Skeet asks in a pathetic stammer.

"It's difficult to say," she whispers honestly after gently guiding him into a hallway strewn with patients in wheelchairs. The smell of age is over-powering.

Don't leave me Skeet! Come back!

"We must be hopeful, though, remember that," the nurse encourages, placing a reassuring hand on Skeet's arm. "Stroke patients have been known to make miraculous recoveries."

Skeet shuffles back to my bedside looking no less strained and fearful. How we had always dreaded the awful day when age and illness would separate us forever. Had that day come?

"It's all right, darling. I'm here. Can you hear me, Tilly? Do you feel me holding your hand?" Skeet softly implores. Turning away so that I can't see him, he sheds gentle tears. But, I see...I see.

Let me out! My husband needs me! Don't cry, darling. Please don't cry. Let me out!

Skeet turns back to me after wiping the tears he can't

2

hide on the sleeve of his faded, wrinkled dress shirt.

"Everything will be all right, Tilly," my husband utters quietly. "You'll be as good as new. You wait and see."

Oh, if wishing it could only make it so. For the first time in my life, Skeet, I don't believe your words. I can't tell you this, but I am sadly resigned...resigned to my confinement in this bed where I can't move or talk. I can only see death and smell its unmistakable odor all around me. I'm trapped in my own body, my own head, only able to think...think about my future of only being able to think. Let's face it. The end for me is probably near...lurking, lurking, lurking. I should think about the past, our past together...yours and mine. Now, that is always entertaining...not a bad way to die, thinking about our past. I picture myself smiling as the memories come flooding back. Am I smiling? Try, try, try...just force it...just...force... it.

"You rest your eyes now, Tilly," Skeet says softly. "I'll be right here, still holding your hand."

That's right. Think about the past. Come with me, Skeet. If I look at you long enough, will you understand my silent plea? Do you remember those long ago days? Can you picture them as I do now? Think back, darling, and remember... remember the secrets, the intrigue...remember those days of suspicion, mystery, and grief...and the worry. I will never forget the worry...or the love. How we have always adored each other. Are you with me, Skeet?

"That's right, my Fig," Skeet says while gently stroking my gray hair. "Close your eyes and relax your mind. Think of nothing else but getting better...and you will."

I am back there again, Skeet. What a time it was in both our lives. Yes, I am back there again...with you.

3

Chapter 2

To Finally Be Home

By my soul, I can neither eat, drink, nor sleep; nor,
what's still worse, love any woman in the world but her.

—Samuel Richardson, *Clarissa, or, the History of a Young Lady*

I slowly shuffled into our modest five-room apartment, thoroughly exhausted after my long trip. Quietly dropping my suitcase to the floor as soon as I crossed the threshold, I walked over to the desk lamp that sat upon the small table in the entryway and turned it on, dimly lighting the entrance that leads into the parlor. I briefly closed my eyes and took in a deep breath. It felt good to be home. Visiting Ma was always a draining chore, but this time around was beyond parallel. She is now safely tucked away in a nursing home, her secrets confined with her...and with me. Last night, on my way back home, I ditched the gun she had used to murder Skeet's father all those years ago after having disassembled it and smashed the pieces beyond recognition. I made a vow to myself right then and there to never divulge to anyone...neither my brother William nor even Skeet...that it was Ma who murdered Sheffield LeMay in retaliation for his unspeakable assault on her when Skeet and I were barely teens. The world was surely a far better place without him... this I knew. I would never feel badly for thinking that, nor would I regret taking my mother's secret to my own grave, a secret that I had decided would not be difficult to keep. And Ma...well...the doctors and nurses at the County Home didn't believe her tortured, confessional ramblings. After all, as far as they were concerned she had lost her mind.

The rest of the apartment was dark as well...and eerily silent. Apparently, Skeet had not waited up for me, but that was okay. It was well after midnight when I walked through the door and I needed the mournful solitude as if the dismal ride home hadn't been enough. I made myself a cup of chamomile tea, slipped off my shoes, and finally sank into the downy cushion of my favorite chair in the parlor. Not yet ready to go to bed, I slowly sipped my tea in an attempt to unwind, but I couldn't stop ruminating. Over and over again flashed Ma's tragic secret in my mind. Skeet would never know that it was my mother who killed his father. Oh, he was well aware that William was his brother as well as mine, a product of one of his father's many "transgressions" as he once put it. He would never hear it from me that the brother to whom he could never reach out because I asked him not to, the brother who I so deeply loved, was a product of something far worse than a mere transgression. And William... well...I was determined that he should remain in the dark, privy to none of what amounted to nothing less than a familial web of tangled intrigues and lies.

Suddenly, the bedroom door opened with a laborious creak, causing the hair on the back of my neck to stand straight on end. My thoughts of Ma's murderous deed and tortured existence were still fresh in my mind. I couldn't turn my brain off to everything I knew, clouding my good sense to recognize the absurdity in thinking that her violent torment had followed me home. I froze to my spot.

"Fig, is that you, honey?" asked a yawning Skeet as he slowly walked out of our bedroom. "I intended to stay up and wait for you, but I couldn't keep my eyes open. How was your trip?"

I immediately relaxed. I was so glad to see Skeet that I quickly placed my tea on the coffee table and went to him, throwing my arms around his neck and giving him a long, passionate kiss.

"I guess your trip was just fine," he said smiling as he gently pulled my arms down and kissed my hands. I looked at him lovingly, feeling so grateful that I had him to come home to.

"How is your mother?" Skeet queried through another yawn. "Still crazy as ever?"

"That's not funny," I snapped, suddenly feeling agitated and vexed by his remark. It was all too fresh and if he only knew what I knew...

"I'm sorry," Skeet said with a smile. "C'mon, honey, don't be mad at me," he chided with his endearing charm as he looked at me adoringly. Of course, I immediately melted.

"William and I placed her in the County Home," I said resignedly. "It was time."

"I'm sorry," Skeet said again, this time in all sincerity. His eyes were downcast. He slowly stroked my hair as his gaze met mine once more. "It's for the best, I'm sure," he whispered softly.

I nodded my head in the affirmative as Skeet placed a finger under my chin and pulled my face closer to his. He kissed me as my tears finally fell and tenderly wiped them away with his hand. I was content to finally be home.

"Let's go to bed," Skeet said, playfully pulling me in the direction of our bedroom.

"But my tea," I started to say, pointing to the mug on the coffee table.

"Forget the tea," he said as he continued to pull on my arm. "I have something much more pressing." His smile was charming...and inviting.

"What can be more pressing than tea?" I said, impishly smiling back.

"Just this," Skeet said, turning dead serious. I knew then that he had something important to say.

"I love you, Tilly, and I need you," he said softly. "I always needed you and I always will. Marry me," Skeet said in a whisper, his eyes burning into mine, "and I'll promise to take care of you for the rest of our lives together."

"We'll take care of each other," I said, smiling tenderly. My heart danced and fluttered.

"Is that a yes?" he asked happily.

"It is," I confirmed, still smiling.

Skeet embraced me and I completely fell into his arms. We would belong to each other forever.

"You're burning up," I commented with concern. "This is the third time this month."

"Always the doctor," he smiled, shaking his head back and forth. "Let's not spoil the mood, honey. I'm fine, " he assured me as he sat me down on the bed and took my left hand. After kissing it tenderly, he placed a diamond ring on my finger. He kissed my hand again, then my lips. I stared at the ring in disbelief and began to cry all over again. Skeet took me in his arms and held me close. His temperature was definitely elevated and I knew it wasn't from the proposal.

"Are you happy?" he asked, smiling that mischievous, boyish smile of his. Taking his hand in mine I smiled back as I squeezed gently. His palm was sweaty.

"I'm so happy, honey," I answered. "So, so happy." I smiled through my tears and embraced him once again.

So, so happy...and so, so worried.

Chapter 3

Frightfully, Frightfully Wrong

It was the best of times, it was the worst of times...

—Charles Dickens, *A Tale of Two Cities*

I didn't want to open my eyes the next morning, but I did...slowly. I was still physically and emotionally exhausted from my trip home, but I had to be at City Hospital early today no matter what. My residency there was grueling, but I knew of no easier way to evolve into the astonishing doctor I had always wished to be. I smiled, though, at the thought of my sweet homecoming the night before. Gazing sleepily at my ring finger, I reached behind my back with my other hand to touch Skeet, but he wasn't there. I turned over and laid a hand on his indented pillow, only to feel the dampness of another night sweat. The sheet was damp too.

"Skeet?" I called out. "Where are you?"

Skeet came out of the small bathroom off the bedroom, wiping his face with a towel.

"Good morning, future wife," he said with a smile as he toweled off the back of his neck.

"Are you all right?" I asked softly.

"I'm just fine," Skeet said, brushing off my comment with a quizzical look as though I didn't need to ask.

He walked over to the bed and kissed me tenderly.

"I'm glad to have you home again," he said. "It was diffi-cult sleeping without you."

Just as he was about to kiss me again, the phone rang.

"Damn, it's only five-thirty in the morning," Skeet com-mented with a growl. "Who in the world could that be?"

I suddenly remembered.

"I bet its William," I said, twisting my face. "I was sup-posed to call him when I got home last night to let him know I had arrived safely."

I picked up the phone on the nightstand and uttered a timid *hello*.

"Oh sure, *now* you pick up the phone," came the light-hearted voice from the other end. "You were supposed to call me when you got in last night...remember?"

"I'm sorry, William," I said, feeling duly chastised. "I meant to call, really I did. It's just that the ride home was so long and unnerving, especially given the circumstances with Ma and all."

"I understand and you are forgiven," William answered cheerfully.

"Besides," I continued, "I would have ended up calling you again this morning anyway. You see, when I got home last night, Skeet proposed."

"Fantastic!" came my brother's outburst from the other end. "Diamond ring and everything?"

"The complete package," I answered with a smile.

"Hey, future brother-in-law!" Skeet shouted as he craned his neck toward the phone. Smiling broadly, he mumbled under his breath, "Brother-in-law, brother...take your pick."

I knew that his sarcasm was all in good fun, but I quickly grabbed his towel and snapped it in his direction anyway, letting out a low-key grunt at the same time.

"Tilly, are you still there?" asked William over the phone. "Are you okay?"

"Yeah, I'm still here, William, and I'm fine. Sorry for the interruption. What were we talking about?" I asked, still feeling clouded over because of the early hour.

"We were talking about your engagement and I'm going to let you hang up now."

William could hear the fatigue in my voice.

"I just wanted to make sure you got in all right last night. And the news about you and Skeet, well, that just made my day. Congratulations."

"Thanks, little brother," I answered. "By the way, what do you have to do so early in the morning?" I asked. "It's only five-thirty."

"Oh, I have to drive over to Leather Junction to meet a seven o'clock train," he said. "Debbie's sixteen-year-old niece will be staying with us for a while. Trouble at home with the parents, you know, that sort of thing."

"Jeez, William, you've just gotten rid of your obligation to one problem. Are you sure you want to take on another?" I asked flat out. "After all, you were the one who took the brunt of Ma's illness you know," I reminded him.

"I have no choice, Tilly. Debbie just informed me last night that the kid would be spending at least two weeks with us, like it or not," William said.

"Charming," I retorted. "What about school?"

"Well, I guess if she stays longer than the two weeks we'll have to enroll her here. Believe me, I'm not happy about it," William stated resignedly.

"Then for goodness sake why in the world are you doing

it?" I asked incredulously.

I really felt for him.

"I'm trying to hold this relationship together, Tilly. You know, start fresh and let things be about Debbie and her family for a while. After having to take care of Ma for so long, well, she feels like she has this coming to her and so do I," William said. "We're kind of raw right now...you know... hanging on to our relationship by a thread."

"It doesn't sound healthy," I said to my brother.

"It isn't," he answered quietly, "but it's all I've got."

"That's not true," I quickly contradicted him. "You've got me and I love you William."

"I love you too," he answered with melancholy.

Skeet nudged me to get off the phone. "You need to be at the hospital in thirty minutes," he whispered. I acknowledged what he said with a nod of my head and a quick wave of my hand after looking at the clock.

"Listen, William, I've got to get to the hospital," I said with urgency. "Let's talk again real soon."

"Okay, but next time you make the call," he said, half joking.

"I will. Promise," I answered. "Goodbye, little brother, and don't forget to take care of yourself," I instructed.

Admittedly, I was concerned about the phone conversation that had just taken place between William and I, and after we hung up I felt badly for him...until I saw Skeet. It was then that the concern I had for William was replaced by downright fear for Skeet. He had suddenly become pale and shaky, holding onto the dresser with one hand while holding his head with the other.

"What is it, Skeet? What's wrong?" I asked in a panic as

I jumped off the bed and rushed toward him.

"Fig, I don't feel so good, honey," Skeet said breathlessly. "I feel like I might faint." He was as white as a sheet.

I guided him over to the bed and sat him down, sitting down myself right beside him.

"What is it, Skeet? I pleaded. "What do you feel?"

"Weak...tired...just bad all over," he said, straining to get the words out as he hung his head over my lap.

His skin was hot to the touch too. Managing to, somehow, look up at me one last time, Skeet uttered, "Help me, Fig," before falling over on the bed and losing consciousness. Something was frightfully, frightfully wrong.

Chapter 4

If She Had Closed Her Eyes

Come what come may, time and the hour runs through the roughest day.

—Shakespeare, *Macbeth*

The drive over to Leather Junction was peaceful enough, but it wasn't something William *wanted* to do, especially without Debbie. She would at least be company on the tedious journey. It was a long trip and the morning sun breaking through the veil of remaining overnight haze was blinding. The road to Leather Junction was an interminable and serpentine thoroughfare, winding its way through the endless hills and valleys that typified the outer fringes of the county. No one else was traveling the road so early in the morning and there was nothing really to look at except for the occasional field of corn or small herd of cattle. The entire excursion was one big bore. But, the fact was that Debbie had to work until midmorning and couldn't make the trip. The positive side of the situation, if one felt so inclined as to identify one, was that Debbie couldn't subject William to the usual harangue about the matters which always seemed to be at hand, such as his job, his insipid personality, and the biggest one...his mother. Oh, it was never a conversation with Debbie, but always a speech that she invariably felt obliged to make while William, for some unearthly reason, felt it his morbid duty to quietly listen. His sheer endurance of Debbie's frequent tirades had to have been born of an unbridled love for the girl. Frankly, his tolerance of her was, well, intolerable...even to another sap.

Leather Junction soon reared its head over the distant horizon blurred by smoke and dust. The train whistle could be heard from the still far off track where the old red and yellow South Central Commuter found its way twice a day, every day from parts near and far. Dooley McQuiggan owned a small coffee shop on the platform while Harper Inkster sold the daily *Junction County Times*, the only newspaper available in these parts. Otherwise, the train station was subdued and almost as boring as the ride it took to get there.

By the time William had gotten to the station, the seven o'clock commuter had come and gone, and his charge was standing on the platform drinking a small cup of black coffee while reading the headline of the day's Times: COUNTY CATTLE DRIVE STARTS TOMORROW.

"It isn't the *Wall Street Journal* is it?" William commented dryly as he walked up to her.

The young girl looked up from her newspaper and coyly smiled without saying a word. Her dark curls and short summer dress had caused William to notice her right away. He most certainly thought she was a cute kid, not unlike her Aunt Debbie when she chose to pretty herself up now and then.

"You must be Christine," William continued. "I'm William."

"I know," the girl said shyly. "I've seen your picture."

"You have?" William asked in astonishment.

"Yes. Aunt Debbie sent my mother a photo of the two of

you about a month ago," confirmed the soft-spoken teen. "Thanks for letting me stay here awhile."

The girl seemed both relieved and cautious at the same time.

"Oh, you're quite welcome," William said with a shy smile. "It's not a problem."

After throwing her luggage onto the flatbed, the two climbed into William's pickup truck and headed out of the train station. At first, the ride was silent and awkward, but when William began to talk about this and that in his typically gentle manner, Christine visibly relaxed and listened to what William had to say with, what appeared to be, genuine interest.

"Have you ever been in this part of the county?" William asked softly after clearing his throat.

"No, I don't believe so," answered Christine as she reservedly smiled at William.

"Well then," William said, suddenly animated, "I'll just have to give you a tour...show you all the pretty spots as we head toward home, okay?"

"Okay," the young girl answered, shrugging her shoulders. "Sounds like a nice thing to do."

William took Christine on a leisurely drive around parts of the county that were well-known, but quite off the beaten track, stopping at Cascade Falls, the Tackle River basin, and a rock formation near the Coniferous Wood that was said to resemble a Kodiak bear. Christine seemed to enjoy the scenery, but refrained from making too many comments or exhibiting much enthusiasm. Finally heading toward home, William felt impelled to comment.

"If you don't mind my saying," he began tentatively, "you

don't seem like the kind of girl who would give her parents grief."

Christine smiled slightly as she gazed out her window, deep in private thought.

"My mom is a nag," she said sharply.

"Is that why you took all those pills?" William asked point blank which was quite straightforward for him.

"You know about that?" Christine asked, half surprised and half embarrassed as she snapped her head in his direction.

"I do," William confirmed, nodding his head.

"Well, I'm sure I won't be nagged at your place the way I am at home," she naively assumed, slowly turning back toward the window to resume her introspective gaze.

William visibly bristled.

"I wouldn't be so sure about that," he said under his breath.

Christine turned back around and looked at William.

"What do you mean by that?" she asked as they pulled up in front of William's place.

He avoided her question.

"Here we are...home at last," William sighed after pulling into the driveway of the apartment he shared with Debbie, a modest two-story house with a tailor shop on the first floor.

Looking at the unpretentious house long and hard, Christine no longer pursued the meaning of William's statement.

"You live in a tailor shop?" she asked, somewhat confused.

"No, we live above it," William said quickly as he needed to say something really important to the young girl before they got out of the truck…something he wouldn't be able to say to her once they got in the house.

"Look Christine," he began gingerly, "you seem like a nice kid. Just remember that your Aunt Debbie means well. She's concerned about your welfare and that's why she asked your ma to let you stay with us for a while."

"I know," said Christine, not quite sure what William was driving at.

"Okay, just so you *know*," said William, punctuating his statement.

Suddenly and with a loud creak, the front door to the house flung open and slammed against the white clapboard siding with a bang.

"Where the hell have you two been?" Debbie shrieked loudly. "It's damn near ten thirty! I've been home for more than twenty minutes waiting for the two of you to show up! Waiting, waiting, waiting!"

Christine looked at William in utter disbelief, for if she had closed her eyes she would have sworn that she had heard her mother's voice. William looked at her sympathetically.

"Welcome to our place, kid," he said with a tinge of sarcasm as they both reluctantly climbed out of the truck. Christine's rehabilitation had begun.

Chapter 5

What We Privately Suspect

I know not all that may be coming, but be it what it will,
I'll go to it laughing

—Herman Melville, *Moby Dick*

"I don't see why I should stay here, Tilly," Skeet mumbled angrily. "I feel fine now."

"You're not well, honey," I said honestly as I stroked his hair, still damp from sweat. "You haven't been well for a few weeks and we need to find out what's going on."

"It's just some kind of flu that won't let go," he said emphatically. "I'm sure I don't need to be in a hospital just to be told something I already know."

"We don't know anything yet, Skeet," I said firmly as I began to feel frustrated with his reluctance to get a definite diagnosis.

Frankly, too, I was damn angry over yet one more unpleasant interruption in our lives. First, William and I had to place our demented mother in a nursing home, and now this. Things had been going along so favorably for Skeet and me...so steadily. Secure in our relationship with the conviction that we were destined to spend the rest of our lives together, we committed to one another without reservation. This undeniable readiness to move forward was a huge and most welcome step, effectively slamming the door on darker days. So, why was this happening now? Why was it happening at all? I wanted to believe what Skeet believed...that he had *some kind of flu*...but my medical training told me something to the contrary. His symptoms were far too chronic and seemed to indicate...

"Good morning, Skeet...Tilly," said a distracted Dr. Trumbull as he walked into the room, flipping through the papers on his clipboard after nodding quickly at each of us.

Flanders Trumbull was a young doctor for whom I had a great deal of respect. He was at the top of his class in medical school and had already earned himself a fine reputation around the hospital as a top-notch diagnostician. I was grateful and relieved to learn that he was on Skeet's case. It was also widely known that he had led somewhat of a charmed life before joining our staff. His parents were so filthy rich that he didn't have to struggle through med school the way I did, financially...or academically; a million dollar endowment to the school from Mr. and Mrs. Trumbull would tightly secure Flan's spot, no matter what his performance.

So at first, Flanders just sort of skipped through his rigorous medical training as though he were romping in a field of wildflowers, trying his hand at a multitude of specializations. By the time he had discovered his passionate interest in both oncology and epidemiology, however, he was deeply committed to being the eminent doctor he is today, thus making his parents' large contribution a good investment. It must also be mentioned that Flan was handsome too, another distinct advantage for him. His dark, curly hair and blue eyes made him an Adonis to whom everything seemed to come quite easily. Yes, Flanders Trumbull had it all and always got what he wanted too...except for the one thing he could never seem to capture...me.

"Good morning, Flan," Skeet answered in an annoyed tone of voice. "When are you going to let me out of here?"

"Not yet, my friend," Flanders answered with a smile. "We still have more tests to run and in case you didn't know it, the paramedics couldn't get you to come around all that quickly on the ambulance ride down here," he said with gravity in his voice. "I'd like you to stick around here for a few days and we'll see what we can dig up, okay?"

Flanders looked at me with his usual captivating expression, waiting for any sign of agreement, or even just faint endorsement, from me. But, all I could do was stare back in stony silence. I was numb from fright.

"Oh, I get it," Skeet started. "The last time you were at our place, you beat me in a game of chess and now you want your money, right? Or maybe you just want to ogle my fiancé some more," he said with a triumphant smile.

"Fiancé?" repeated an astonished Flanders who appeared to have turned a bit pale.

"That's right," I chimed in softly with a proud smile. "Skeet proposed last night."

Skeet took my hand in his as we both looked at our friend who had clearly been startled by the announcement.

"Well then, I guess congratulations are in order," Flanders conceded.

His smile was slightly begrudging, but he shook Skeet's hand heartily.

"I wish the two of you a wonderful life together," he said.

"That was the plan," said Skeet. "Will it be a long life, Flan?" he asked. "Should I return the diamond?"

"Skeet," I whispered quietly as I nudged his shoulder.

"Oh, don't return that diamond yet," said Flanders with a smirk as he looked at me. "You have to have faith you know."

Faith was the key. Ma would have said so too...if she still had her mind.

I glanced out of the large hospital room window to watch the rain come pouring down. The dark, stormy day mirrored my exact feelings.

"So," Flanders continued, "it says here that you've had a number of fevers."

"Yeah, maybe three or four times over the last couple of weeks," Skeet calculated inaccurately. "No, make that five or six times," he said, correcting himself.

"Any unusual weakness or fatigue?" Flanders asked.

"Some," Skeet said, making it sound inconsequential.

"Skeet, be honest," I said quietly, gently nudging him again.

"Okay, lots," he admitted, once again correcting himself.

"What else?" Flanders asked.

"Night sweats," I interjected quickly, "and he's been complaining about feeling aches and pains all over his body."

"Now I told you, Fig, that my aches were brought on by my job. It's grueling work, you know," he said, feeling compelled to remind me of his daily physical activity on the construction site.

"I understand that," I said, "but the job isn't responsible for the five pounds you've lost in the last week."

"Well, the fevers killed my appetite," Skeet reluctantly confessed. "Whatever this virus is," he whispered wearily while shaking his head, "it just won't let go." He let out a prolonged sigh.

In the meantime, Flanders was taking copious notes.

"Do you think it's a flu virus, Flan?" I asked, knowing full well that he couldn't possibly know the answer to that yet.

"Tilly, it very well could be," he said, patting my arm. "Like I said, I have a few more tests to run. Be patient."

He raised an eyebrow and continued to write.

As I stood next to Skeet's bed, I placed my hand on his shoulder. He looked at me reassuringly, but I felt uneasy about the situation, having already dismissed in my mind any notion that he may have contracted the flu. This I did not convey to Skeet, but the expression on my face must have been telling.

"Don't worry, honey," Skeet said. "Everything will be just fine."

He reached up and placed a hand on top of mine while smiling sweetly. I bent down and kissed his lips gently. At that point, Flanders excused himself.

"Close your eyes now and rest," I whispered in Skeet's ear. "They'll be running all sorts of tests soon and you'll be poked and prodded throughout most of it. You'll need your strength."

"Will you be with me, honey?" he asked as though he were a small boy.

"I'll be right there with you," I assured him. "I'll even hold your hand and give you a lollipop."

"An all day cherry sucker?" he quietly chuckled, his eyes now closed.

"If that's what you want, darling," I whispered in his ear.

Skeet was slowly drifting off to sleep.

I seized upon the moment and ran out into the hallway after Flanders who was standing by the nurse's station at the end of the long corridor. As I began to walk toward him, it felt as though my feet were weighed down with something heavy, something meant to purposely hold me back. Everything around me became surreal, pulsating in rippling waves that were slow to move. As though I were walking through the misty convolution of a bad dream, every step forward seemed to put me farther back. I couldn't reach Flanders quickly enough as sheer anxiety took hold. As I approached in breathless distress, he looked up from his papers.

"Flan, come clean with me," I said, finally close enough to confront him. "What do you think is wrong with Skeet?"

I couldn't be more straightforward than that and he could sense that I expected an answer.

"Well, like I said," he began tentatively, "it might just be a nasty flu virus..."

"Stop right there," I interrupted in exasperation. "Do you *really* think we're dealing with a virus? I don't."

"I have thoughts to the contrary too," Flanders admitted honestly, "but that's all they are...just thoughts...nothing confirmed. So please, Tilly," he requested curtly, "let me run my tests. I have learned to never tip my hand without confirmed results...not even to a friend."

He looked back down and continued the intent study of his papers.

"Obviously you have some thoughts of your own," he remarked quietly, never picking up his head.

"I do," I said firmly.

"Would you care to share your thoughts?" he asked, looking up again from his papers.

"I don't dare utter them for fear they might come true," I

said in earnest. "The *medical* side of my brain thinks scientifically, but the *country girl* side always thinks superstitiously. Perhaps if I don't dare speak of what I'm thinking, then maybe this entire nightmare will go away."

"That's one of the things I always loved about you, Tilly," Flanders commented frankly. "You're both brilliant and folksy at the same time. So, let's both just listen to that folksy side," he said gently, his tone of voice far more compassionate than it was before, "and keep our thoughts to ourselves, shall we? Let the test results, whatever they may be, do all the talking, okay?"

"All right, Flan, I'll agree to that," I said. "There's no point in jumping to conclusions."

I continued to feel anxious which was now compounded by disappointment. I should have known better than to expect Flanders Trumbull to let me in on his thoughts at this early stage, especially since he had no confirmed test results. God forbid he should ruin his fine reputation for my sake. And why should he? After all, Skeet's proposal had startled him, effectively forcing the realization that I could no longer be even a *possible* conquest. Why should he engage in a speculative conversation that would only serve to temporarily appease *me*? This, I soon understood, was clearly out of the question for a doctor of Flan's caliber. I could only hope that what we both privately suspected...was not true.

Chapter 6

The Worst Possible News

*All happy families are alike; each unhappy family is unhappy
in its own way*

—Leo Tolstoy, *Anna Karenina*

Only several days had passed, but to Christine it seemed like an eternity. Now she knew what William meant, what he was *trying* to tell her about her Aunt Debbie but couldn't. She felt as though she had never left home, as though she were living with her mother all over again...nag, nag, nag.

"And I'll tell you this, girl," snapped Debbie as she proceeded with her early morning lecture, "it is never a good thing to hang around with the wrong crowd. If you do that, you might as well resign yourself to the fact that there will eventually be trouble. Trouble, trouble, trouble. And that is certainly what you've earned yourself—a *peck* of trouble. Whoever allowed you to have the sort of friends that you do was wrong. Wrong, wrong, wrong. They're nothing but a bunch of delinquents and that's exactly what you'll become if you stay with them. Then what? What will happen to you? Where will you go? What will you do? Who would ever be able to love a girl like you... take care of a girl like you? You need to think, Christine, but you haven't been thinking. That's part of your problem. You haven't been thinking or using any semblance of good judgment. It's a shame.

Shame, shame, shame."

"I don't mean to interrupt, Aunt Debbie," Christine quickly interjected, "but I have a headache."

"Well, *that* came on out of the blue," declared Debbie with a twisted look on her face. "You want to know what I think? I think you know I'm right and you don't want to hear what I have to say anymore...you don't want to listen to good reason. That's *another* part of your problem, Christine. You don't listen. You must listen, listen, listen," Debbie scolded, pounding her fist on the kitchen table.

"No, this headache has been coming on ever since I got out of bed this morning...really," Christine asserted, calmly standing up to her prickly aunt. "I think I'll just go back to bed and sleep it away," she said quietly as she turned back toward her bedroom, only to be shamed into stopping.

"Go back to bed!" Debbie shouted. "For Christ's sake, you just got up! That's another thing that's *wrong* with teenagers. They don't face their problems head on. They just crawl back under the covers like worms in the dirt. Crawl, crawl, crawl."

To Christine's relief, William walked into the kitchen from the other room, curious as to what the heated discussion was all about. She looked at him gratefully.

"What's going on in here?" he inquired with a furrowed brow.

William looked from Debbie to Christine and then back again as he waited for an answer to his question. Knowing Debbie, he had no doubt that the wait wouldn't be long.

"I'll tell you what's going on in here," Debbie said, practically biting William's head off. "Little missy here thinks that she's going back to bed...says she's got a *headache*. Well,

27

she might as well know right now that that isn't the way things work around here, is it William? She needs to take a couple of aspirin and face her problems head on like a normal human being. Tell her, William. Tell her what she needs to do. Tell her right now."

Debbie was practically frothing at the mouth.

William looked at Christine with great empathy and she quickly picked up on that. She smiled at him weakly and he smiled back...ever so faintly. It was difficult to know whether or not Debbie had noticed their commiseration.

"You're not feeling well?" William asked Christine while trying to appear disinterested.

"No, I guess not," she answered. "I have a headache and it's getting worse."

"Well," William began with good intent, "I would say that if you feel *that* poorly then you should head on back to bed. You probably only need to get a few more hours rest."

William knew that what he had said would incur Debbie's wrath, as all of his comments lately seemed to rub her the wrong way, and he was right...Debbie was absolutely fuming with anger, this evident in her twisted expression and red complexion.

"Thanks, William," Christine said quietly.

She got up from the kitchen table and walked out of the room without so much as glancing at her aunt.

As soon as Christine's bedroom door closed, Debbie brought her fist down on the table once again.

"How dare you," she seethed. "Who do you think you are telling my niece to do something that I clearly did not want her to do? Ever since you dumped your mother into that County Home you've been ignoring my wants. The impudence! You haven't listened to a word I've said in days. Whenever I talk to you lately, your eyes simply gloss right over or you just look off into the distance!" Debbie screamed while flinging her hand in the direction of a distant place that was nowhere in particular. "I'll tell you what happens to people like you, William; they wind up alone. That's what happens... alone, alone, alone!"

William stood in the kitchen doorway and listened to Debbie's tirade. He smirked as he walked over to the stove and poured himself a cup of coffee. Was it worth it to say something back to her, given the further scene it would cause? William didn't ponder that question too long. Despite Debbie's difficult nature and rough disposition, he still loved her...thorns and all.

"You know something, sweetheart," William began, "I'm on *your* side...I always have been. Now, I'm committed to helping you straighten Christine out but from where I stand, she seems to be just a sweet and lonely girl who needs some kindness and understanding. Hell, you're riding her so hard that she might as well be back home with your sister who was treating her the exact same way. Isn't that why she swallowed all those pills? You've got to lay off a little bit, honey. Give her some breathing room," William valiantly concluded.

Without giving Debbie a chance to lecture him for his response, William walked out the back door, closing it behind him. Before Debbie could chase after him in a fit of rage, which she most certainly would have done given her temper, William opened the door again, only to stick his head in.

"And Deb," he interjected, causing her to spin back

toward him with an icy glare, "don't you ever mention my mother in one of your diatribes again."

And with that, William quietly shut the back door, rendering Debbie speechless.

What neither of them knew was that Christine had opened her bedroom door a crack to listen to the entire exchange. William was her protector, she thought, her guardian angel. He would watch over her and help her to work out her problems, insecurities, and self-esteem issues. At long last, she felt as though she had found someone who actually cared about her feelings and she, well...she cared about his feelings too. Christine's headache had gone away, only to be replaced by butterflies in her stomach. She smiled and with tempered jubilance closed the bedroom door.

Suddenly, the telephone rang.

"Hello," snapped Debbie. "Yeah, he's here. Hold on."

After tossing the telephone receiver onto the kitchen table, the cord immediately recoiled, sending the dirty, yellow receiver crashing to the floor.

"William! Phone!" Debbie screeched out the back door before quickly turning on her heels and stomping out of the room.

William came back into the kitchen after having sat on the back staircase in silent triumph. At first, he looked on the kitchen table for the receiver, but then followed the stretched out cord with his eyes to the floor. There it lay, still squirming like a snake. Shaking his head, he snatched the receiver off the floor and sat down at the table.

"Hello?" William said, trying to untangle the snarled cord with his other hand. "What? Oh no...*oh no*."

William bowed his head and rubbed his eyes.

"No, I'm here," he said quietly. "Thanks for calling. Yes, I will. Goodbye."

William was stunned and immediately turned ashen in color. It was bad news...the worst possible news. With the phone still off the hook, making that beeping sound that it always makes after the connection has been broken, William quietly laid his head down on the kitchen table, closed his eyes and let out a long, throaty sigh. Could this day get any worse?

Chapter 7

A Lightning Bolt Out of the Blue

If you live to be a hundred, I want to live to be a hundred minus one day,
so I never have to live without you

— AA Milne, *Winnie the Pooh*

"I've been lying in this bed for three days," complained Skeet, "with nothing to show for it. I've been poked with needles over and over again. I think they took half my blood, honey," he whined to me. "What the hell is going on?"

"We don't know yet," I said resignedly, "or, at least, we're not sure yet."

"What do they *think* it is, Fig?" Skeet asked. Damn, they took a bone marrow sample last night, now *that's* serious, isn't it?"

I could hear the panic in his voice.

"Skeet, Flanders is covering all of his bases by performing so many tests," I told him reassuringly. "Every test that comes back negative will, in effect, eliminate that particular disease from the list of possibilities until the field is narrowed down to the one specific thing that has inflicted you...whatever it may be. Unfortunately, it is the only way to be thorough. Try to understand, honey, and please be patient with the process."

"Am I dying, Fig? Just tell me flat out. I can take it," Skeet said firmly as he squeezed my hand in his.

His eyes burned right through me and revealed a mix of anger and fright.

"Be honest with me, honey," he pleaded in a softer tone. "I deserve to know."

"You're not dying, Skeet," I assured him. "We're actually lucky that Flan is your doctor because he's being so thorough and extra cautious...as always. That's why he has such a good reputation. Not only will he pinpoint exactly what's wrong, but he'll fix it too."

I laid my cheek on top of his head and held on to his hand.

"Don't worry, darling," I said softly. "We'll have our wedding and a good, long life together too."

"That's what I want, Fig, more than anything else in the whole world," Skeet said. "It's my *dream* for us to be married...maybe have some kids."

I looked at him and felt such a deep love and devotion. I didn't want to believe...wouldn't let myself believe...that we might be dealing with something more serious than a virus. I shuddered at the thought.

"I want us to have a nice house with a garden," he continued sleepily as his eyes began to close, "and I want to dance on our fiftieth wedding anniversary."

"You don't know how to dance," I jibed, chuckling softly. "You have two left feet, remember?"

"I'll take lessons," he smiled faintly before falling sound asleep.

Poor Skeet. He was physically and emotionally drained.

I walked out into the corridor, not as a doctor but as a frightened fiancé. It had never occurred to me that I might be sitting on the other side of that invisible fence one day...

the fence that separates the doctors from the families. Ma...
well...she is a different case altogether. She is so tortured
and mind twisted that William and I knew exactly what we
needed to do...no questions, no fence. It was a relief when
we settled her into the County Home because we were all on
the same page. But this...this was a lightning bolt out of the
blue.

"How are you holding up, kiddo?" asked a benevolent
Flanders Trumbull as he walked up to me in the corridor,
placing a hand on my shoulder.

"Okay, I guess," I answered gravely. "I don't have the
heart to tell him that I suspect something serious...and I
believe you do too."

"I'm afraid it has gone beyond suspicion, Tilly," said Flan.
"Let's talk in there," he said, pointing to the room where we
take families to break bad news.

My legs turned to jelly. I couldn't bear to learn what I
already knew.

After Flan and I talked for what seemed to be an eternity
in slow motion, I walked back into the corridor in a daze. For
some strange reason I thought of Ma again, maybe because
her tragic story was so fresh in my mind and still so painful.
Or maybe it was because I was reaching out to her for comfort as though I were a little girl again. What would she have
said to console me? What would she have done to soothe my
aching heart?

I somehow made my way to the hospital chapel where I
sat on the far end of the last pew. It was dim and private,
allowing me to close my eyes and gather my thoughts. Flan
and I both agreed that I would speak to Skeet before he did.
Once I broke the news, he would be in to inundate us both

with all the jargon and minutia of the diagnosis. How would I tell him...without breaking down?

I closed my eyes and thought back to the days when I was a young girl and Ma would take me to the little white church on Sundays where she would fervently pray...enough for the both of us, I suspect. Ma knew that I was never one to pray, but in spite of that she always urged me to talk to God anyway. The scientific side of me adamantly scoffed at prayer, *and* God...silently, of course, for fear she would throttle me for my heathenish views. She knew me well enough, though, to discern that deep down inside I *did* believe in God, and I *did* pray...in my own way...without even knowing it. In her infinite wisdom, she allowed me to grow into my beliefs in due time at my own pace. Her only demand was that I attend church every Sunday without complaint. If I didn't want to pray, then I should just sit quietly; God would find his way into my heart.

Well, here I am God, sitting quietly. Can you hear me? Can you find your way into my heart? Please, God, don't let anything happen to him. Please. I am begging You...begging for his life. If you take him, You might as well take me too.

My eyes pooled with tears that fell quickly down my cheeks. I wiped them away on my sleeve and stood up.

I guess you can say I prayed, God. Did you hear me? It's me...Tilly.

I turned and walked out of the little hospital chapel, stunned and trembling. I had not derived the comfort from praying the way that I thought I would...the way that Ma always did. I wasn't ready to talk to Skeet either, but I had no other choice. He had to know.

Besides, I would *never* be fully ready to tell him this

news.

I walked toward his room as though I were trapped in a nightmare. No other news had ever affected me so deeply. Despite that, it was time to pull myself together and be strong...for Skeet's sake. Hadn't I been trained to convey bad news to patients using just the right bedside manner? I had indeed...but not to *this* patient. I reached the door to Skeet's room and took a deep breath.

"Hi, Skeet," I said with a brave face. "Did you have a nice nap?"

I bent down and kissed his forehead. It was warm.

"Hi, Fig," he said tentatively as he studied my face. "Your eyes are red. Have you been crying?"

He took my hand and stroked it as though he were trying to soothe me.

"What is it, honey?" Skeet asked. "Have they found out what's wrong with me?"

"Listen, sweetheart," I began tentatively, the words sticking in my throat. "Your test results have come back."

I did my best to keep my voice from quivering.

"Now that we know what we're dealing with, we can tackle it head on with every available treatment," I continued, forcing an upbeat voice as I tried to put a good spin on things, still avoiding the actual words he needed to hear.

"And just exactly what is it that we're dealing with?" Skeet demanded to know.

He searched my face for an answer, looking for any sign or clue.

"Honey, you have leukemia," I finally said, breaking it to him as gently as I could.

He stared at me in disbelief.

"You mean it isn't a virus?" he asked. "I don't have the flu?"

"No, honey," I said with regret that pierced my soul, taking his hand into both of mine and caressing it tenderly.

Skeet closed his eyes and laid deeply into his pillow. A lone tear trickled down one cheek as he slowly shook his head from side to side. In a hushed voice, he repeated the same word over and over again.

"Damn...damn...damn."

Chapter 8

At Rest Now

Life's but a walking shadow, a poor player that struts and frets his hour upon the stage and then is heard no more: it is a tale told by an idiot, full of sound and fury, signifying nothing

—Shakespeare, *Macbeth*

As William's head lay on the kitchen table he began to cry. He cradled his face in his two trembling hands, effectively muting his uncontrollable sobs. How could this be? How could it have happened?

He heard the sound of light footsteps in the kitchen as though in a dream. They were not enough to distract him from his grief, though, as he continued to cry while still hiding his face in his hands. His tears were plentiful, stinging his increasingly irritated eyes and soaking his palms, as they slowly trickled down his cheeks and into his mouth. Even a faint awareness that the beeping telephone receiver had been picked up off the kitchen table and placed back on the hook didn't prompt him to raise his head. A gentle hand stroked his hair and then rubbed his back, calming him down considerably, as he began to pull himself together. As he felt his shoulders being tenderly massaged, a soft breath skittered off the nape of his neck, tickling him ever so slightly. Thank goodness, he thought, that Debbie was no longer angry with him. He would need all of her love and support now. As always, he was ready to forgive and forget.

"Don't cry, William, please don't cry. What is it? What has happened?"

William froze to his spot. Something was terribly amiss... inappropriate...even creepy. He immediately stopped crying and, with an overpowering apprehension, looked up to see a concerned Christine standing over him. He suddenly felt a cold shiver run down his spine.

"Where is Debbie?" William asked brusquely, feeling overwhelmingly embarrassed that he had appeared so vulnerable, so exposed in front of the teen.

"I don't know," Christine shrugged matter of factly. "I haven't seen her. What is it, William? Why were you crying?"

Christine was genuinely concerned for him, but also curious. She had never seen a grown man cry before. This, however, didn't give her license, William thought, to be so...forward.

William looked at her with a tinge of fear, and for good reason. He considered her touch to be almost sensual, certainly not that of a teenage girl but, rather, that of a woman who was, suffice it to say, well rehearsed.

"I've had some bad news," William said as he abruptly stood up from the kitchen table and slowly backed his way to the nearby wall, never taking his eyes off of Christine.

"I'm sorry to hear that," Christine said softly as she walked toward him. "Is there anything I can do to...alleviate the pain?" she said in a whisper, carefully measuring her provocative words as she stood directly in front of William, close enough for him to feel her warm breath on his face.

William looked at the wispy teenager who possessed the allure of a woman. He hadn't been seduced in a very long time and had almost forgotten what it felt like. But this was wrong...wickedly wrong. When Christine slowly brought her young face forward in an attempt to kiss William, he quickly placed his hands on her shoulders and gently pushed her back, affectively rejecting her lascivious overture. What she really needed was a good scolding, but he hadn't the emotional strength to give her the real trouncing she so richly deserved. Nevertheless, he would make his feelings known.

"That's not a good idea," William said sternly as his eyes burned into Christine's. "You didn't come here to get into more trouble."

She searched his face for any sign of weakness, but it just wasn't there. William had fended her off, rejecting her advances outright.

"Who's getting into more trouble?" Debbie bellowed as she stormed into the kitchen.

"No one," William said curtly. "No one is getting into more trouble."

He spoke pointedly and resented Debbie's continued crass behavior. He shouldn't have to deal with it...not today.

Debbie looked at him long and hard as though she were searching his face for a lie and then turned to Christine, searching her face as well.

"Who was that on the phone?" she inquired icily, her eyes still trained on Christine.

Debbie's expression clearly conveyed suspicion and an obvious distrust of her niece...and William.

"That was the County Home," William said quietly as he picked up the telephone to dial his sister. "Uh, yes. Would you please page Doctor Matilda Figlit? That's right. It's an emergency. This is her brother."

Debbie turned her eyes from Christine to William, glaring at him in cold curiosity.

"Ma's dead," William finally blurted out after noticing her frosty expression. "She died in her sleep. They think it was a heart attack. Are you satisfied now? I know you never liked her."

Debbie seemed to soften her posture toward William as she immediately relaxed her angry countenance, this exposing a tamer side that rarely showed...especially lately. She told William that she was sorry, but not without cracking a slight smile after he looked the other way while on the phone. To her, William's deranged mother was a burden who had lingered on this earth far too long. As for Christine, she just stood there in awkward silence.

"Hi, Tilly," William began. "I've got some bad news."

***

Once again, I made the long ride home after William called me about Ma's death, this time having bad news of my own. My emotions were so terribly mixed, but my feelings of stress and anxiety over leaving Skeet alone and sick in a hospital bed haunted me most of all. Of course, I then felt tremendous guilt because my fears over Skeet's health took far greater precedence in my mind than my sorrow for Ma's passing. The entire situation was so surreal. What rotten timing!

"I'll be back in two days," I promised Skeet. "William will surely understand."

I knew I would have to recount Skeet's diagnosis to William, which would compound the sadness of our mother's death for him...and for me...all over again.

When I arrived, I told William everything as we made plans to bury our mother. He was both shocked and disheartened by the sudden turn of events.

"I can't believe this is all happening at once," William sighed sadly. "I know that, somehow, we'll get through it. But right now, we are both so completely consumed by trouble and heartache that it seems to me our problems are without end."

"Oh, they *will* end, little brother," I said definitively, placing my hand on his shoulder. "You have to believe that...we both do."

I only hoped that I could heed my own words.

I met Christine for the first time and made polite chitchat with Debbie—the kind that was superficial and barely tolerant; she didn't even have it in her to express her sympathy to me. I knew that Debbie and my brother had a contentious relationship...certainly not the kind worth keeping, in my opinion, since they weren't even married yet. Why start off a marriage on the wrong foot, having to scratch and claw your way out from the deep, dark abyss of irreconcilable differences? My brother didn't know it yet, but his relationship with this girl was going nowhere fast. I paused to think, and trembled at the faint parallel I could draw between them and Skeet and me. After all, we weren't in any position right now to plan a new life together either, through no fault of our own, of course. I quickly put those thoughts out of my mind, knowing in my heart of hearts that one day soon Skeet and I would see good times again.

The plan for Ma's burial called for quick and simple action. She would be in the ground within two days in a remote section of the County Cemetery with a few kind words, prayers, and blessings bestowed upon her resting place by the newest reverend from the little white church. Besides the reverend, William and I would be the only two people there. That was how we both wanted it. A memorial service would properly honor Ma in the not too distant future but for now, all I could think about was getting back to Skeet. I prepared to leave...again.

"I'm sorry it has to be this way," I said mournfully to my brother. "I wish I could stay longer, but I just can't. I'll be back for the memorial service, and I'll let you know what's going on with Skeet as soon as I can."

"Let's talk on the telephone every day," William said anxiously.

I agreed and hugged my brother hard. This time, I our parting would be difficult for the both of us.

"Tilly, she's at rest now, isn't she?" William asked, looking for reassurance.

"Yes, William," I said firmly, looking into his eyes. "She's at rest, at total peace."

"No more demons?" he asked.

"No more demons," I answered in a whisper, placing my hand on his cheek.

Only I could ever know why those demons had Ma in their vicious grasp. Sweet death had kindly liberated her, sending them and the shackles that chained them to her tortured soul crashing straight to hell. I could only hope that Ma wasn't dragged down there with them.

Chapter 9

Resigned to the Inevitable

Hand to hand is how it will be, a life and death fight against the fiend, and

he whom death bears off shall submit to the judgment of the Lord.

— Beowulf

"I thought you'd never get back, sweetheart," Skeet said, breathing a sigh of relief as I anxiously walked into his hospital room. "I was so worried about you. Are you okay?"

He took my hand and kissed it tenderly.

"*You* were worried about *me*?" I asked as I bent down to kiss him. "I'm fine. Ma is finally resting," I said mournfully.

"I'm so sorry, Fig," Skeet said sympathetically. "I would have given anything to be there with you...to support you."

He smiled faintly and continued.

"You know, I have some fond memories of your mother too. She was a tough lady," he commented, slightly nodding his head in the affirmative, "but she understood, from the very beginning, how we felt about each other. She was always on our side."

He mustered another feeble smile as his eyes pooled with tears. It seemed as though he was genuinely mourning Ma's passing, but he certainly had reasons of his own to be melancholy. I would never know if my mother's death was the actual reason behind this show of emotion, as I didn't want to question him. I simply smiled back in appreciation for his sweet words about Ma and gently stroked his hair. It felt damp.

"You do support me...every day," I assured him. "How are *you* feeling today?" I asked, quickly turning the table on our conversation.

Skeet's health was my number one priority and I wanted him to know it. Even Ma's death couldn't change that.

"The same," Skeet said in a matter-of-fact tone. "Flan said that he was going to explain..."

Just then, the good doctor walked into the room, right on cue.

"Ah, Tilly," Flan said softly. "You're back. You have my deepest sympathy."

He was a man of few words, but his tone was compassionate and sincere.

"Thank you, Flan," I said soberly. "Skeet just told me that you were going to explain...something."

Flanders pushed his eyeglasses up to the bridge of his nose with his index finger. As he cautiously shuffled and reshuffled his papers, he cleared his throat before answering me.

"Well, what I want to do right now is explain the entire situation as succinctly as possible before outlining my treatment plan. Of course, either of you may interrupt me at any time," the young doctor stated. "OK?"

I took Skeet's hand and swallowed hard. I supposed that now would be as good a time as any to find out just how far his leukemia had advanced. At any rate, the treatment plan would inevitably place him on a long, long road to recovery.

"Okay, Flan, we're ready," I said, breathing deeply as I smiled warmly at Skeet.

His eyes widened like those of a small child.

"The leukemia you have, Skeet, is quite aggressive," the doctor began. "What's happening here is that your bone marrow isn't working properly. You see, the stem cells inside the marrow have been adversely affected by the disease, so they are producing abnormal cells."

"Abnormal cells?" Skeet repeated with trepidation.

"Yes, and what I mean by abnormal," Flanders continued, "is that your body isn't producing healthy white blood cells anymore which is wreaking havoc on your red blood cells as well. These diseased cells are prolific, thus crowding out any normal blood cells you may have and, therefore, making you sick."

"I see," Skeet said thoughtfully. "Am I going to die?"

His startling question honestly conveyed his alarm, but it wasn't the first time he had brought up the subject of dying. I bristled and squeezed his hand.

"That is, at no point, a part of my plan," Flanders stated quickly as he waved his finger. "I believe that a treatment plan far more aggressive than the leukemia itself will keep us a step ahead of it and, effectively, put the disease into remission...permanently."

"Are you telling me that I have a chance?" Skeet asked.

"You have more than just a chance, my friend," said the doctor. "But, I won't lie to you. If you agree to my treatment plan, it is going to be a long, hard road."

Skeet looked at me with an expression that conveyed both fright *and* a longing for protection from all that was about to happen to him. There was nothing I could do. I felt completely helpless.

"Let's hear your plan, Flanders," I said calmly.

"Well, now I'm sure much of this will sound familiar to you, Tilly, but if you have any questions, or even any suggestions, just interrupt me," Flanders said.

I deeply appreciated his inclusiveness.

Flan's words were well rehearsed and he spoke with, what can almost be called, an excitement. I had often heard that once the young doctor made a diagnosis he became thoroughly energized and dynamic, ready to roll up his sleeves and eradicate the problem...whatever it may be. Some even said that the sicker the patient was, the more animated Flanders Trumbull became. No lowly disease would ever be allowed to sully the reputation of *this* medical whiz kid. He would aggressively attack it as though he were a rabid animal...every time. That certainly lent itself to his stellar reputation as a doctor. And no one could ever argue with his success rate. It was exemplary.

"Okay, it works like this, Skeet. You will start off with chemotherapy and radiation treatments in extremely high doses," Flanders said.

"Isn't that dangerous to the bone marrow, Flan?" I interjected quickly. "His marrow may stop making any blood cells at all."

"That is absolutely true," said Flanders. "I find that in most cases like this where the treatment is acutely aggressive, the bone marrow ceases to work altogether. However, we have found that these elevated-dose treatments have a much higher success rate than the standard-dose treatments when attacking and killing cancer cells."

"But he needs those blood cells that his bone marrow produces in order to survive," I said with concern, not telling him anything that a first year medical student wouldn't already know. "How do you plan on getting around the fact that your treatment plan will probably destroy his bone marrow?"

Skeet was engrossed, not saying a word. He intently looked back and forth between Flan and me as though he were watching a Ping-Pong match. I squirmed uncomfortably in my chair. I knew what Flanders Trumbull was going to say next.

"Well, that's where a bone marrow transplant would come in," he said in earnest.

"A bone marrow transplant?" Skeet reiterated.

I closed my eyes and gently shook my head back and forth. This nightmare had just taken on a whole new dimension.

"Yes. It is really rather straightforward," said Flan, "and the success rate is quite high."

I could see him getting excited again as he explained to Skeet just how the procedure would work. I was suddenly engulfed by nausea.

"You see Skeet, the transplanted cells would replace the body's source of blood cells after the bone marrow has been destroyed by the high-dose treatments. These transplants allow doctors to use much higher doses of chemotherapy at the outset because in the end, we know there is a viable way to repair the damage."

"Yes, but we also know that they can have serious risks too," I cautioned. "Patients can die from complications."

"That's true enough," Flanders acknowledged, "but I believe that in this case, the benefits to Skeet's health would far outweigh the risks. As a matter of fact, we know that donated cells find and kill cancer cells much better than the immune cells of the person with the cancer ever could. This is an incredible benefit."

"Really?" Skeet chimed in excitedly.

"Oh, yes," Flanders said with conviction. "You see, certain types of transplants actually help to fight the cancer rather than just simply replace defective blood cells. Amazing, isn't it?"

Flanders looked as though he were comfortable with the presentation he had just made, and extremely confident in his plan. I wasn't so sure about it, though, as my mind began to race. After all, Skeet didn't *really* understand the transplant process because if he did, he would certainly bristle at its probable ramifications, not to mention the familial complications it would bring about. I panicked and held my breath.

"I say we do it," Skeet said, interrupting my thoughts. "The sooner we get started on all of this, the better."

"Hold on, Skeet," I quickly warned. "We can't rush into any of this. What Flan is proposing can be extremely risky."

I shifted uncomfortably in my chair again as I held his hand.

"Are there any alternatives, Flan?" Skeet asked, seeing how uncomfortable I was with the treatment proposal.

"Well, there are the lower-dose treatments, of course, but in my professional opinion, your chances for remission would be much slimmer. The lower-dose treatments would drag on for much longer in your case, and I have my doubts as to whether they would be effective enough to keep us ahead of the disease. As I said, we need to be aggressive."

Flanders looked at me with questioning eyes. He didn't understand my reluctance...my dread.

"What do you think, sweetheart?" asked Skeet. "I really don't think I have a choice."

"Oh, Skeet," I said, my eyes filling with tears. "You don't understand."

"Please know, Tilly," Flanders interrupted, "that the stage of Skeet's leukemia, his age, and overall good health make him a perfect candidate for my plan. I believe that it can work, but we must start right away. His health will deteriorate rather quickly if we don't."

I was somewhat in shock, but resigned to the inevitable. Above all else, Skeet had to overcome his disease...no matter what.

"All right, Flan," I reluctantly conceded as I looked at Skeet with concern. "Move forward with whatever you think is best for him."

"That's my girl," Skeet said with a forced smile for my benefit. "Okay, Flan, where do we begin?" he asked.

"Well, I'll schedule the chemotherapy treatments right away. Then we need to get a jumpstart on your transplant donor," Flanders said decisively as though he had done this a thousand times before.

I cringed.

"The donor must have a tissue type that closely matches yours," he continued. "We'll start by looking at a close family member. The odds of a match are usually pretty good, but if that doesn't work we'll just look for a non-related donor."

Skeet suddenly realized what was being said. His jaw noticeably dropped as he gave me a frightened glance. My stomach flipped. *Here it comes*, I thought.

"So tell me, Skeet," Flanders began, "do you have a sibling?"

Chapter 10

You See...Here's the Thing

She is a mortal danger to all men.

— *Edmond Rostand,* Cyrano de Bergerac

"She's gone now and that's good for us," Debbie said coldly. "We can finally breathe without worrying about your mother and her twisted visions of dripping blood and other conjured up nonsense. Frankly, I'm glad it's over."

"You're being heartless, you know that?" William shot back. "She was ill...a tortured woman. Can't you find it in your heart to be the least bit charitable toward her now that she's gone?"

"Hell no," Debbie said definitively. "We haven't had any kind of a life together because you were always with your damn mother."

"She couldn't be left alone," William said in a soft, far-off voice. "She was so afraid of...everything."

The memory of her sad, final days filled William with grief.

"Well, I say we go out for drinks, have a nice dinner, and forget the last few years ever happened," Debbie said, insensitive to William's anguish.

"But they *did* happen," William said pointedly, "and they swallowed my poor mother right up. She went completely insane! What did you expect me to do? Leave her by herself? Let her face all of those nightmares alone? That would have been cruel and heartless...impossible for me to do...impossible!"

Just then, the door to Christine's room opened, and the teen silently walked out into the kitchen...undetected.

"What I *expected* you to do was stand up for yourself...for us...to that no good sister of yours," Debbie spat out. "She got off, free *and clear*, from having to do a damn thing for your crazy mother while you always had to be over there holding her hand, cooking her meals, or putting her to bed," Debbie enumerated caustically.

William stood up quickly from his chair, knocking it to the floor.

"I could strangle you for what you just said," he blurted out angrily. "She was my mother! I had no choice! And as for my sister, she was in medical school. She did what she could!"

William was seething with rage over Debbie's ruthless, pitiless tirade. He could not believe how blatantly callous she had become, how cold-blooded. It was particularly barbarous, even for Debbie. Could he *really* love such a woman?

"Don't ever bad mouth my sister again!" he commanded loudly as he continued, bringing his fist down hard on the kitchen table. "If it weren't for her, I'd go insane too!" he shouted, feeling so incensed...so provoked.

William's entire body shook with fury. It was all he could do to prevent himself from putting his hands around Debbie's throat. Had it actually come to *this*?

At the same time, both William and Debbie suddenly realized that Christine had walked into the kitchen and stood herself quietly in a corner, intently listening to the entire toxic exchange. The girl was duly horrified, but couldn't take her eyes or ears off of the two battling adults. It was so strangely alluring...like watching a train wreck unfold.

"How do you like that, Christine?" Debbie shouted sarcastically upon seeing her niece. "Your future uncle just threatened to kill me. You heard him say it."

"I don't think *that's* what he meant," Christine said quietly.

The young girl took a deep breath.

"You should try to be a little nicer, Aunt Debbie," she admonished softly, knowing that her statement would incur her aunt's wrath. "He just lost his mother."

"Well, aren't you the little smarty pants," Debbie said tartly. "Mind your own damn business or you can just turn yourself right back around and head on home to your mother."

Christine glared at her aunt and then slowly turned to William, searching his face for any sign of support.

"C'mon, Christine," said William. "I'll drive you over to the County Post so you can mail that letter you wrote to your mother."

"No, you will not drive her *anywhere* right now," ordered Debbie who, by this time, was spitting rusty nails. "We still have a few matters to iron out."

"Go on and wait in the truck, Christine," William quietly instructed.

She reluctantly left the kitchen...and him.

On the one hand, Christine felt as though she should stay to back William up in case he should need it, but on the other hand, she sensed that he did not want her in the middle of this fight. The young girl could not quite make up her mind as to whether William should be considered loyal, even noble, for staying with Debbie...or just plain stupid.

"So, what matters in particular need to be ironed out right this very moment?" William asked Debbie with obvious scorn, his hands on his hips.

"You told me," Debbie began through clenched teeth, "that as soon as your mother was placed in a nursing home, you would run out that very same day and buy me an engagement ring. Well, here we are!" she shouted with outstretched arms. "You and Tilly *did* place her in a nursing home, but I never got that ring! Then, your sister got a diamond from that sickly boyfriend of hers, and *still* there was no ring for me! Finally, I figured I'd get my ring after your mother up and died from that heart attack, but here I am... *still...without...a...ring*! I'd say that makes you a liar. Now, what do you say about that?" Debbie growled, stomping one foot.

William visibly gathered himself and answered Debbie in what could be considered an extremely cool, calm and collected manner, given all of the awful things she had just said...and the vicious way in which she had said them.

"You're absolutely right," William began, his sudden composure taking Debbie by surprise. "I *did* promise you an engagement ring and I never followed through on that promise. And yes, Ma did have twisted visions of dripping blood and other conjured up nonsense and because of that, our life together these last few years has been limited...I guess you can even say nonexistent. As for my sister, I never demanded that she give me more help because I knew she wasn't in a position to give it to me. I did all of the hand holding and the cooking for my mother; I put her to bed and slept on her couch in case she woke up with nightmares; I followed her around the backyard to make sure she didn't fall into the creek behind the house...and I put our life together, yours and mine, on hold because my mother needed me."

Debbie eyed William with a triumphant glare. At last, he understood that she was right, and that he had been so very wrong all along. Wrong, wrong, wrong.

"I'm glad you finally realize just how *terribly* you've been treating me," Debbie victoriously stated, "and just how wrong you were to give your mother all of that attention without so much as giving me..."

"Hold on," William interrupted, furrowing his brow. "I never said I was *wrong*. I did what I had to do for my mother because that's what families do."

"Oh, is *that* what families do, William?" Debbie asked sarcastically. "Well, what about *our* family? Are we ever going to start *our* family?" she asked, completely exasperated.

"You see...here's the thing," William began without hesitation. "I think if I really wanted to marry you, I would have given you that ring by now. I just don't think we're right for each other."

His words were bold and sincere. William had finally unburdened himself...and it felt gratifying.

"You promised that you would take care of me!" Debbie shouted. "I've been robbed and stepped over like some drunk in a dark alley!" she seethed, pointing her finger in William's face. "If you think I'm going to let *you dump me*, then you have another thing coming!"

"My dear," William stated calmly, "you have just *been* dumped. Get the picture?"

Debbie was shocked. She had never experienced such an unfeeling attitude from William before, not to mention the sudden assertiveness of late that was so unlike him as well. The unmitigated gall!

After hearing what he had to say, Debbie suddenly began to swing her fists at William, aiming to strike his head, chest, and arms. She did not land a single punch, however, as William successfully ducked every swing, eventually grabbing her two wrists.

"William?" came a soft voice from the kitchen doorway.

Christine had been silently standing in their presence once again, having gone undetected for at least a minute. She acted as though she were magnetically drawn to the physical altercation, her jaw slightly dropped in astonishment, but her ears highly perked in fascination nonetheless. William looked over his shoulder as he struggled to hold Debbie's arms down.

"What do you *want?*" he asked, more than a little out of breath. "I told you to wait in the truck."

"Well, I *was* in the truck, but then someone pulled into the driveway," Christine said, mortified for William. "I ran up here to tell you that...well...you have company."

***

I stepped out from behind Christine after having climbed the long set of stairs leading to the second floor. I looked at my brother curiously as I walked into the apartment and unbuttoned my overcoat. William had a tight grasp on Debbie's wrists, but the two had ceased to struggle upon seeing me. Debbie's rage remained obvious, though, while

William's breath continued to be short and labored.

"Have I come at a bad time?" I asked, raising my eyebrows a little while stuffing my hands into the pockets of my coat. The question was certainly a rhetorical one, as I already knew the answer. Oh brother...what next?

Chapter 11

Mighty Big News

Nothing is so painful to the human mind as a great and sudden change.

— Mary Shelley, *Frankenstein*

After Debbie had scraped the small amount of dignity she had left off of the floor, she slinked out of the kitchen into her bedroom and loudly slammed the door.

"I'm sorry you had to see that," said an embarrassed William as he hugged me. "What are you doing back here so soon? Is it Skeet? He didn't..."

"Well, it *is* about Skeet," I began as I sat down at the kitchen table. "He's resting comfortably right now, but his doctor has made it clear that he will need very strong treatments to knock this thing out. It's not going to be easy for him," I lamented.

"How are *you* holding up, Tilly?" William asked, placing his hand on my shoulder. "Between Ma's death and this, you have a lot on *your* plate too. Are you ready for whatever may lie ahead?"

"I wouldn't say that I'm exactly *ready* for it," I began honestly. "This whole thing has been such a shock that I'm still trying to process through it. I guess the best thing to do is to take it one day at a time. That's what I always tell my own patients."

I was sadly resigned.

"It sounds as though you should listen to your own advice," said William. "It's good stuff."

Just then, Christine, who was still standing in the doorway of the kitchen, cleared her throat as if to remind William and me that she was still in the room.

"Oh, Christine, I'm sorry," William apologized, raising his hand to his forehead. "I'll bring you to the County Post later on...if you don't mind," he trailed off.

"I'm sorry to interrupt what you two were going to do," I said, looking at Christine. "It appears that I've come at a bad time. That brawl looked to be very..."

"It was a long time in coming," William said with a quick wave of his hand, cutting my sentence short. I'll deal with her later."

He looked absolutely disgusted.

"I think I'll just take a walk," Christine said awkwardly, her presence now an intrusion. She slipped through the kitchen door and quickly descended down the back staircase.

"Okay, Tilly," William started cautiously, "what's up? You didn't drive all this way to give me news that you could have given over the phone."

"Well, I was wondering if there have been any nibbles on Ma's house," I said, delaying the inevitable.

"No, not yet," said my perplexed brother, "but it hasn't been on the market that long."

William looked at me suspiciously as I got up from my chair and began to pace the floor.

"Okay, spill it," he finally said. "Something is wrong and I want to know what it is...*right now.*"

He was adamant.

I took a deep breath. This would probably be the most difficult thing I ever had to say in my entire life.

"William, Skeet will probably need a bone marrow transplant," I said with a cringe, getting it out as quickly as I could.

I knew my revelation was just the tip of the proverbial iceberg because there was so much more I had to say...and expose. Nevertheless, William's eyes widened at the startling news, never expecting it to lead to further shock and upset. Everything within the parameters of what he knew to be true was about to be destroyed. I dreaded what I had to tell him, what I promised myself he would never find out as long as I was alive.

"Wow, Tilly, that's serious," he said in disbelief. "What does Skeet have to say about that?"

"Oh, he's all for it," I confirmed. "Naturally, we're *both* hopeful that it will work for him."

"Well, that's mighty big news," William said, raising an eyebrow and shaking his head. "Whatever I can do, you just let me know."

He didn't know the half of it.

William felt badly for me and, in fact, regretted deeply the entire situation, this I could tell. He liked Skeet very much... he always did.

"As a matter of fact there is something," I said.

"Name it," responded my brother.

"Oh, damn it, William," I blurted out in frustration. "No more beating around the bush."

I sat back down at the kitchen table and took my brother's hand.

"We'd like you to consider becoming a possible...no, change that to a *probable* bone marrow donor for Skeet's transplant," I said flat out.

"Me? Why me?" William asked, visibly taken aback by my request.

"We need your stem cells, little brother," I said, looking intently into William's eyes.

"Tilly, I'm willing to do whatever I can to *support* the two of you, but don't you think you're asking a bit much of me?" William gently admonished. "I mean...doesn't the hospital have a list of donors for cases like this? I'm sure there is someone out there who is completely willing..."

William was rattled.

"Yes, but *their* antigens may not match *Skeet's* antigens," I interrupted him.

"Their what?" my brother queried.

"Their human...leukocyte...antigens," I responded slowly.

"Well, what makes you think that *my* human something or other would be a good match? True, I've known Skeet for a lot of years, but our blood is worlds apart."

"Not true," I cringed again.

I secretly hoped that William would guess what I was trying to tell him so that I wouldn't have to say the words myself, but that was wishful thinking on my part.

"What do you mean by that?" William asked curiously. "Are you trying to tell me that Skeet and I have the same blood? And how would you *know* that without some kind of test anyway?"

I pursed my lips and squeezed William's hand hard.

"I know that because...Skeet is your brother," I said steadily, successfully keeping my voice from quivering...to

61

my surprise.

I felt as though I would faint, though.

"My what?" William asked as though he were in a fog. "Did you say...my brother?"

"Yes," I confirmed, "that's exactly what I said."

William got up from the kitchen table, his turmoil and bewilderment betrayed by his expression. He walked over to a corner on the other side of the room and quickly turned back around to face me. He then put his head down and walked to another corner...then another...then another...as though he were an animal trapped in a cage.

"What the hell are you talking about, Tilly?" he finally uttered, the words sticking in his throat.

I had to tell William the entire gruesome story: how he had been conceived in violence because Ma had been assaulted by Sheffield LeMay; how that made him Skeet's half brother...and *my* half brother too; how Ma insisted on raising him as though he had the same father as I did, while burying her terrible ordeal deep, deep inside the recesses of her mind; how Ma loved him so very deeply, despite who his father was, and how neither she nor I ever, ever intended for the awful truth to come out.

William's jaw hung low, rendering him speechless.

"I'm so sorry to have to tell you all of this now, William," I said, feeling just awful and somewhat selfish. "It's just that I need you...Skeet needs you. You may be his best chance... his only chance...for survival. Please understand."

My words were measured and heartfelt, but William was clearly reeling. Who could blame him?

"Understand?" William said with a quivering voice. "You're the one who needs to understand, Tilly, that this changes everything...who I am, who *we* are, and where I came from. Everything was a lie...everything."

"Not everything, William," I said softly. "It wasn't a lie that Ma loved you very much. It isn't a lie now that I love you too and no matter what, you are my little brother."

William was breathing heavily, his hands on his hips.

"Where is he now?" he asked as though he would go out and kill Sheffield LeMay on the spot.

"Who?" I asked, making believe I didn't know who he was talking about.

"Sheffield LeMay, who else?" William snapped. "I've often heard you speak of Skeet's mother, but never his father. Where is he?"

I froze. Should I tell William the *complete* truth about how Ma had murdered Sheffield LeMay all those years ago for what he had done to her? And how *that* is why the poor woman lost her mind? Do I dare divulge who I alone knew to be Sheffield LeMay's murderer when I vowed to take that secret with me to my grave?

"He's gone, William," I asserted. "Dead and buried. It happened a long time ago."

"What happened?" he persisted. "How did he die?"

"I believe he was murdered," I said cautiously as though I weren't quite sure.

"Murdered?" William repeated in disbelief. "By whom?"

He was determined to know the truth, firing one question after another.

"I don't think they ever caught his killer," I shrugged. "The case went cold many years ago and has never been solved. All I really remember about him is that he was a vile, despicable man."

"Obviously," my brother shot back with a palpable loathing.

William looked at me in stone cold silence for what seemed to be an eternity, and then, without a single word, stormed out of the apartment.

"William!" I shouted after him. "Please come back! Please!"

His nerves were understandably raw after having learned the true identity of his father and the despicable circumstance under which he had been conceived. I could only hope that in time, after the awful revelation had thoroughly sunk in to his head, William would see his way clear to helping his brother.

The sudden sound of screeching tires pierced the air. I looked out of the back kitchen window to witness a large, billowy plume of dust left in the wake of William's fishtailing pick up truck. Where he was headed I had no way of knowing. He certainly had a lot to think about, to digest. As of now, I could make only one assumption. William had just fled...from himself.

Chapter 12

Something Positive

It is far better to endure patiently a smart which nobody feels but yourself, than to commit a hasty action whose evil consequences will extend to all connected with you; and besides, the Bible bids us return good for evil

— Charlotte Bronte, *Jane Eyre*

At first, William drove aimlessly about, navigating the winding back roads of the county's most rural areas with reckless abandon. His tires screeched as though voicing the pain he felt so acutely in his heart. He couldn't help but relinquish all self-control as he started to cry, causing his chest to heave in spasm. William's blood boiled with an anger that he had never experienced before, while his eyes held pools of tears that blurred his vision. For a fleeting moment he thought that if a tree appeared close enough to the roadway he might feel strongly inclined to steer his pickup truck straight for it. How was it that his mother could have deceived him for so many years? In finding out about this horrible secret now, he felt as though she were reaching out from her grave with both hands and strangling him breathless. He had never been victim to a more heart wrenching shock. It was now, in the midst of his agony, that he found himself talking to his dead mother.

"Why didn't you tell me, Ma?" William repeated through his sobs over and over again. "Why didn't you tell me? Why...didn't...you...tell...me?"

Blue skies hung for miles as warm breezes gently embraced the county like a friend, making the day exceptionally pleasant; this a sharp contrast to William's mood. He felt lost, not of this earth. What Tilly had told him cruelly pulled the rug out from under his world. After a lifetime of being raised as the William he thought he was, a horrible identity shift now made him someone else, someone most peculiar. Who was this depraved man who attacked his mother, this cowardly monster who took advantage of a defenseless woman? His singular repugnant act altered William's view of everyone and everything he considered to be inviolable. He now regarded his very existence as an aberration.

All roads led William to the remote section of the County Cemetery where he pulled up to his mother's roughly chiseled headstone. It simply read:

Eugenia Figlit

Wife and Mother

William stared at the stone for a long while, his emotions raw and churning wildly. He slipped out of the truck and slammed the door. With his hands in his pockets, he slowly took the few steps to the modest grave where he stood and pondered. His emotions were mixed but the anger, resentment, and sheer astonishment over Tilly's revelation undeniably overshadowed the love and devotion he had in his heart for his mother. She was the victim. Why should he be so angry with her?

Well, let's see now, William thought carefully. *She lied to me throughout my entire life as to the actual identity of my father. She perpetuated the lie by allowing me to think that I was a certain someone when I was really someone else. At the end of her life, I took care of her unconditionally and without regret to the detriment of my own well-being and personal relationships, never knowing that I had been duped... tricked...fooled by my own mother. I'd say that's enough to feel...to want to...*

Without further provocation of thought, William kicked his mother's headstone off of its foundation and knocked it to the ground. His chest heaved once again as his breathing became uneven and shallow. He looked down upon the stone that lay flat in the grass, his mother's name facing up to the heavens, and slowly shook his head back and forth before hanging it low. William closed his eyes tight and clenched his teeth for a good long while before coming to a decision.

Knowing that he could never allow himself to live in anger, resentment, and bitterness for the rest of his life, William resolved then and there to somehow come to terms with the entire atrocious situation. What else *could* he do? He had to find a way to reconcile his feelings and move on. Was it possible to turn the awful truth into something...*positive*? Maybe it wasn't too late to find that out.

William knelt down with sad regret and picked up the felled headstone. Luckily, it hadn't chipped or cracked. He firmly planted it back on its foundation and anchored it securely.

"I'm sorry, Ma," he said out loud, "for everything I've been thinking. I love you still."

William gently patted the stone and turned away, sluggishly walking back to the truck with his hands in his pockets and his head bowed, ashamed of what he had done... what he had thought...about his poor, pitiful mother.

Feeling much calmer and more collected, William drove down the main county road toward home. His shame over the cemetery incident subsiding, he mulled over in his mind exactly what he would say to his sister and how he would say it. Her awful revelation aside, she had asked something of him...something extraordinary... that needed a response. It was this that he thought about as he headed for home, now an inalterably different William.

As he drove and pondered the weighty situation in which he found himself, William suddenly saw Christine sauntering along a nearby grassy knoll, picking wildflowers. He immediately pulled off to the side of the road and rolled down his window.

"Want a ride?" he asked somberly.

Christine picked her head up and smiled immediately upon seeing him. She quickly made her way off the small hill and jogged toward William's truck, the petals of her wildflowers dancing slightly in the mild breeze. She stood next to the driver's side door, her heart aflutter at the sight of him outside of the apartment, away from the toxic atmosphere... away from her aunt. She thought he must have come out to look for her.

"Where are you headed?" she asked with a smile.

"Home," William said definitively. "I have some business to settle with my sister."

"You always seem to be settling business," Christine said with a pout. "When do you have fun?" she asked flirtatiously.

"There isn't much in the way of fun going on right now... in case you haven't noticed," William said sarcastically.

"Well, I don't know if I *should* go home with you right now," Christine said teasingly. "Given everything that's been going on, I feel just *wretched* there," she moaned as she brushed a wisp of William's hair back into place with the tips of her fingers. He grabbed her wrist and cast her hand aside with an unexpected force. Christine was taken aback. Sooner or later, William thought, she would get the message that he wasn't up for grabs.

"Suit yourself," he said, not caring much about the girl's feelings at that point...or whether or not she got into the truck. "Be home by supper," he ordered as he rolled up his window and quickly sped off again toward home.

Christine glared in the direction of the speeding truck and the billowy plume of smoke and dust it had left in its wake. She shrugged her shoulders and sauntered back to the grassy knoll, thinking that William would be a tough nut to crack.

As he pulled into the driveway of his apartment, William noticed with a sense of relief that Tilly's car was still parked in the same spot. He took a deep breath and got out of the truck. Could his sister ever forgive him for running off when she needed him most? If he had stayed, he would have eventually realized that he must reconcile his feelings like a man, and that did *not* include pushing his mother's headstone over, an incident he would recount to no one. If he had not been so self-absorbed in his own shock he would have quickly acknowledged what his sister was trying to tell him—that Skeet could die without his help. If that were to happen, how would he ever be able to face his sister again? There was no point in agonizing over who his father was any further...this he now clearly understood. He wouldn't allow his outrage over this shocking revelation to cause a tragedy from which neither he nor his sister could ever recover. This was his opportunity...the perfect time to turn the awful truth into something positive.

***

I could hear William's familiar footsteps coming up the back staircase to the apartment. He walked quietly into the kitchen where he found me sitting at the table reading a magazine. Our eyes locked and I breathed a sigh of relief.

"You're back," I said. "Thank God."

"Okay, I'll do it," William blurted out.

"You will?" I said, surprised and relieved.

I smiled gratefully at my brother and threw my arms around him, hugging him long and hard.

"I will," answered William confidently as he lovingly hugged me back. "I'll do it for you and..."

William's eyes were cast downward as he backed up, and his smile was almost...bashful.

"For me and who else?" I gently asked.

"For you and...my *brother*," William said, still smiling as he looked up at me.

He wasn't yet used to the fact that he even *had* a brother but at that moment, William had turned the awful truth into something...positive.

Chapter 13

A Far Cry From Where We Started

Be strong and courageous. Do not be terrified; do not be discouraged,
for the LORD your God will be with you wherever you go

— The *Bible*, Joshua 1:9

Skeet began the long, dreadful days of intense treatment. He had been itchy to get started, yet frightened of the difficult journey he would have to make toward recovery. It would be honest to say that none of us, not even Flanders Trumbull, *really* knew what the extent of that journey would be...or just *how* it would end. An aggressive treatment plan had been put into place, specifically designed by Flanders to knock Skeet's leukemia into permanent remission. This would be the all-consuming goal.

Initially, his blood was put through a filtration process before chemotherapy even began, lowering his blood counts immediately and significantly.

"That process just blew my counts out of the water," Skeet excitedly said to me. "Can't we just call it a day?"

"Be patient, honey," I said, stroking his arm gently. "This is just the beginning. You'll get through it all, though," I reassured him. "You'll get through it all."

It *was* just the beginning because *that process*, as he called it, would be effective for only a short while. It would buy some time, though, before the chemotherapy started and had a chance to effectively kick in and do its job. It was really quite a fascinating yet simple procedure, the key to getting off to a good start. First, his blood was removed through an intravenous tube and passed through a special machine that removed white blood cells and leukemia cells. Then, the blood that remained was returned to him through a different intravenous tube. Skeet found this to be tedious.

When the chemotherapy actually began, we braced ourselves for the unpleasant side effects. Only periodically did I leave his side to do this chore or that. Hospital administration had notably lightened my own duties, allowing me to be with Skeet much of the time. My mind wasn't exactly on my work anyway. Just as Flanders Trumbull had promised, Skeet's treatment was intense.

"He is young and in general good health," Flan kept saying. "He'll tolerate it all right...you wait and see."

And tolerate it he did, never complaining once. I think he was more worried about me than anything else. The only thing he seemed to be anxious about was William's reaction to all of this.

"He's willing to be a transplant donor if you need him," I told Skeet.

"Does he know what happened between my father and your mother?" he asked in a tired voice.

"He knows," I said. "It's out in the open now. He knows you're his brother."

"And he'll do this thing for me?" he asked in a whisper, his eyes closed.

"Yes, he will, sweetheart," I reassured him. "He is standing by, waiting for our call."

After having said that, Skeet fell fast asleep.

Naturally, Skeet's treatment was aimed at getting rid of as many leukemia cells as possible, but Flan knew that William was his ace in the hole.

"I feel even more confident now, knowing that we have a sibling waiting in the wings," Flanders said.

That certainly did not diminish the intensity of the prescribed treatment. During the first phase of the chemotherapy, typically called induction, Skeet had to take no less than three different kinds of drugs for about a week. Just as Flan had predicted, the drugs destroyed his normal bone marrow cells as well as many of the leukemia cells. Skeet developed dangerously low blood counts and became extremely ill. He needed antibiotics and two blood transfusions. He also needed a drug to raise his white blood cell count.

"I'm going to die, aren't I?" he asked me weakly through his mask.

"You are *not* going to die," I said gently but firmly. "You *must* believe that. Be strong...fight, fight, fight," I urged him on.

"I feel really bad, honey," he said in a throaty whisper.

"I know you do," I empathized, "but you'll feel better...I promise."

First off, I doubted my own words, never having seen him *so sick.* Secondly, I had told myself not to make him any promises. *For Heaven's sake, get on your game, Tilly.* What was wrong with me?

Skeet's blood counts stayed low for a few weeks. He remained in the hospital, of course, and became quite bored as he gathered some strength. That, I thought, was a good sign.

"I hate this place," he said.

"That's understandable," I answered sympathetically.

"All I can think about is going home...to sleep in my own bed, use my own toilet, take my own shower, and look out of my own window. When can I go home, Fig?" he pleaded like a small child.

"Soon," I told him. "Very soon."

At least he wasn't talking about dying anymore.

At this point, Flanders did a bone marrow biopsy.

"Let's try a bit more chemotherapy," he directed, after which time came another biopsy.

"Just what I suspected would happen did, in fact, happen," said Flanders, never missing an opportunity to highlight his omniscience. "There are still leukemia cells in the bone marrow...a bit of a higher percentage than what is considered acceptable...but I *am* encouraged."

My heart sank as Skeet drew in a deep breath. All I heard was, *still leukemia cells...higher percentage than what is considered acceptable.*

"What does that mean?" I asked impatiently. "Didn't any of the treatment work at all?"

"Oh, it sure did," said Flanders, nodding his head. "His leukemia cells now comprise only about eight percent of his bone marrow, a far cry from where we started. He's not *too* far off the acceptable mark of five percent, but because his initial white cell count was so high, I would say that a bone marrow transplant is unavoidable. I *could* do another round of chemotherapy, but that would only delay the inevitable."

"Are there any *normal* bone marrow cells returning?" I asked.

"There are," answered Flanders, "and they are beginning to make new blood cells right on cue. However, I fear that those cells will be overtaken rather quickly as the leukemia cells that remain begin to multiply...and they will do so at a fast rate. You must allow me to initiate the transplant process immediately."

Skeet and I looked at each other.

"I guess it's time to give William a call," Skeet said resignedly.

"It'll be the most important phone call you ever make," said Flanders. "As we discussed before, a transplant will reduce the risk of the leukemia coming back more so than the standard chemotherapy ever could. It offers you the best chance for long term survival."

"What is the downside to a bone marrow transplant, Flan?" asked Skeet in earnest.

"Well," Flanders began thoughtfully, "there are short term side effects but as I've said before, transplants are *also* more likely to cause some *serious* complications that chemotherapy treatments alone would never evoke, including an increased risk of..."

"Death," Skeet chimed in. "Right?"

"Well, yes," said Flanders, "but *that* is not going to happen to you. Like I've said before, it is, at no point, a part of my plan."

"How do you know that we can avoid it?" Skeet asked honestly. "The grim reaper isn't picky."

"Because I am Doctor Flanders Trumbull, *that's* how I know," he answered, cock-sure of himself. "And you need to know too."

Flan pointed a friendly finger at Skeet before turning to leave the room. He gave me a smile and thumbs up as I watched him briskly walk out into the long corridor, off to his next case...his next challenge.

I leaned back in my chair with a more hopeful outlook, given Flan's certitude. I thought back to the day I first met him, the world already groveling at his feet. I had never met another doctor with more self-possession...or a greater success rate. Undeniably, he had finally roped me in. If there was ever a doctor who could get Skeet out of this mess, it was Flan...I was certain of that now...and I could only hope that Skeet felt the same confidence that I did. At any rate, I was sure that Flan would have no trouble drawing Skeet in... hook, line, and sinker...if he hadn't done so already. Having his patients in the palm of his hand, thoroughly convinced in his abilities to cure them, was an integral part of his charisma, his medical magic. There was no doubt in my mind whatsoever that Skeet and I could *both* believe that this would all work out. After all, Doctor Flanders Trumbull was on the case.

Chapter 14

Off the Hook

The only people for me are the mad ones, the ones who are mad to live, mad to talk, mad to be saved, desirous of everything at the same time, the ones who never yawn or say a commonplace thing, but burn, burn, burn like fabulous yellow roman candles exploding like spiders across the stars."

—Jack Kerouac, *On the Road*

"I'm Doctor Flanders Trumbull," he said conceitedly, as though I should drop everything I was doing and genuflect.

"I'm Doctor Matilda Figlit, but my friends call me Tilly," I answered with well-matched confidence and a smile.

His eyes burned right through me while he smirked as though I should have *known* who stood before me, even without the introduction. Actually, I already knew of Doctor Flanders Trumbull and so did everyone else on staff. He had a reputation as a ladies' man but he also did more than just commendable work, making him the envy of every other young resident in the hospital. He knew that too...and reveled in it.

Doctors who had been on staff for years couldn't get over just how well this rich kid from "up north" was able to diagnose an illness with pinpoint accuracy and remedy the situation every time, even though he was barely out of medical school. It didn't matter what type of illness it was either. There was the elderly nun who had contracted rabies after having hand fed the nipping squirrels behind her convent; the senator with typhoid who had drunk contaminated water while on a goodwill visit to Borneo; the grocer with trichinosis who liked to nibble on raw pork when the butcher wasn't looking; and the professor with malaria who insisted upon living and teaching in a remote area of Africa while neglecting to update his vaccinations. As if those cases weren't enough for the young doctor's dossier, there later came the ballroom dancer who returned home from a competition in the Caribbean with tuberculosis; the crossing guard with anthrax who had secretly lived in an empty shack on the grounds of a tannery; the great-grandmother who contracted the plague while keeping wild rodents as pets; and the out-of-work snake handler who took a job as an attendant at a kennel for feral dogs and cats, only to wind up with Rocky Mountain spotted fever. Finally, I would be remiss if I forgot to mention the race car driver who was thought to acquire leprosy through his life-long hobby of trapping armadillos. The list went on and on.

Then, of course, there were your average, everyday members of the general populace with run of the mill cancers, respiratory diseases, and blood disorders who seemed to flock to Flanders Trumbull in droves for a miracle cure. There was no disease too acute, no virus too persistent, and no infection too pervasive that couldn't be successfully treated by the good doctor. Once, an admiring nurse sarcastically asked him if he could walk on water, thus spawning the nickname Doctor Jesus to which he was never really adverse, but just merely pretended to be. Yes, he had a reputation as a golden boy...and the fat head to go along with it.

Although he expected reverence, even capitulation, not *everyone* swooned at the sight of Flanders Trumbull...including me. This peppered his eagerness all the more to charm and conquer me. To his continual annoyance, though, I ignored his self-serving agenda time after time, never once acquiescing to his overtures. Truth be told, I found him to be completely...resistible.

"I suppose you'll want to sit at my lunch table today since I'll be discussing my diagnosis of the little girl who was helicoptered in from that mountain town," he haughtily said to me once.

"No, thank you," I answered quickly as I juggled my paperwork. "I have a pretty heavy schedule myself today, so I doubt that I'll even have *time* for lunch."

I continued to scurry about with my paperwork after which time I walked over to the supply closet to take an inventory of the stock, my least favorite job at the hospital. Flanders followed me right into the small, walk-in space.

"Well, if you can't listen to what I have to say at lunchtime then you'll definitely want to have dinner with me tonight," he arrogantly assumed. "You really shouldn't miss out on what I have to say."

"I am subjected *every day* to what you have to say," I shot back, mildly aggravated. "Will you please step aside so that I can count the number of tongue depressors on that shelf?"

"You don't like me much, do you?" Flanders asked me with a crooked smile.

Given that I knew the young doctor was insincere and an unabashed skirt chaser to boot, I didn't have the faintest desire to become another notch on his stethoscope, despite his gifted abilities to save the world from deadly disease and illness. Besides, I was unquestionably committed to Skeet... the only man for me.

"It's not that I don't like you, Dr. Trumbull," I said sincerely. "It's just that I have a boyfriend. We live together and our relationship is exclusive."

I brushed past him quickly as I made my way over to the bandages and sutures.

"Oh, you *live* with someone," he said, a bit surprised. "Well, that never stopped a gal from keeping company with me before...in a purely innocent and platonic way, of course," he said, tongue in cheek.

"Of course," I said facetiously.

He laid his arm across the shelf, making it impossible for me to pass.

"I promise to show you a good time," Flanders said in a low, seductive voice, almost as though he were mocking himself.

"I have all the fun I can stand...at home...with my boyfriend," I said, emphatically driving the point across.

"Suit yourself," he said, shrugging his shoulders and conceding defeat. "I'd like to meet this boyfriend of yours. Maybe he can teach me something in the way of..."

"Charm? Sincerity? Modesty?" I interrupted.

"All right, all right," Flanders said with a wave of his hand, getting my point.

I knew right then and there that he wasn't a bad sort but probably a lonely one, given the fact that none of his relationships were genuine. He was an exemplary doctor, though, and not so deeply buried was an honorable man too...in spite of his vanity.

"Would you like to have dinner with Skeet and me...say Thursday night?" I asked.

"Really?" he said with surprise in his voice. "Sure! I'll bring the wine."

Flanders smiled broadly, thoroughly delighted to accept the dinner invitation. I then suddenly wondered if he had any friends at all, this man who was always surrounded by people but seemed to be so lonely for company.

"That's fine," I said, "but I must warn you that after a couple of glasses of wine, Skeet will be bound and determined to rope you into a game of chess."

"I *love* chess," Flanders said.

"So does Skeet," I answered with a smile.

"And he loves you too," he said, suddenly turning serious again.

"Unconditionally," I nodded in reply, staring at him with a deep conviction in what I was saying.

"Well then, I guess I know where I stand," Flanders admitted while backing up, placing his hands on his hips.

"May I ask you just one more question?" he asked soberly.

"Sure, what is it?" I said, breathing in deeply and expecting one last come-on.

"Red or white?" he inquired as the look on his face was brightened considerably by his broad smile.

"Excuse me?" I said with a confused look.

Not having heard the flirtation I anticipated, his question completely through me off.

"Red or white...*you know*...meat or fish?" he asked lightheartedly.

We both chuckled as he helped me move a large box of surgical gowns to another shelf.

"Red, I guess," I said. "And remember to bring your best chess gaming strategy. Skeet will be out for blood," I commented with a smile of my own.

"I will," Flanders said, "and Tilly...thanks for the invitation."

He was sincerely grateful.

"You're entirely welcome," I answered.

And I meant it. He and I now had an understanding... and a mutual respect.

Ever since that time, the three of us have been fast friends. Flanders Trumbull never attempted to hit on me again, although Skeet knew full well that he had done so in the past. Now, we needed his friendship...and his expertise...more than ever. And in exchange for that, I made a vow to remain eternally in his debt...if he could get Skeet...off the hook.

Chapter 15

Hell Hath No Fury...

Lord, what fools these mortals be!"

—Shakespeare, *A Midsummer Night's Dream*

William came home from work that one dark day, the heaviness of the still air indicating an impending storm certain to be intense, only to find most of his clothes and other various belongings on the front lawn of the tailor shop. Debbie had been a screeching shrew all morning long, according to Mr. Analdi Pantaloni, the good natured tailor who not only owned the shop, but the rest of the building as well.

"The clothes were showering down in front of my shop window," said the nervous landlord, raising his arms up and then lowering them slowly while wiggling his fingers to imitate a raining effect.

William clearly got the picture.

"There were socks in the bushes and shirts in the trees. When I walked out to see what was going on, I got hit on top of the head with a wristwatch. Mama mia! I thought the department store in town had exploded!"

Ever since William had informed Debbie that he had no intention of marrying her, she made it her business, her singular goal in life, to make him regret his decision.

"*You* broke it off with *me* after I showed nothing but patience...patience, patience, patience," she spat out as she pointed a finger in his face. "So, if you think that I'll be the one to move out of the apartment...then think again," she ordered viciously. "I'll be damned if *you* put *me* out on the street. You should be the one to leave...leave, leave, leave!" she ranted and raved...on and on and on.

William calmly but firmly informed Debbie that *she* would be the one who would have to move out.

"After all," he reminded her, "I *am* the one who pays the rent around here, and it was *you* who moved in with *me*."

He maintained a steady voice and never lost his composure.

"I lived in this apartment a full year before we even met," he said. "This is *my* place. It would be best if you just pack up your belongings and go back to your folks."

That brusque statement, William's definitive dismissal of the girl, drove his point across like a slap in the face, sending Debbie into another tizzy. She would never allow herself to be humiliated by having to move back home with her parents. No, she was determined to stay put. However, as William began to make preparations to leave his apartment above the tailor shop and travel to City Hospital to help Skeet, he informed Debbie in no uncertain terms that she should follow his advice. He wanted her gone by the time he got back...or he would get the sheriff to throw her out.

"I'd say that's fair," said William. "It gives you *plenty* of time."

And so it did...to make mischief, that is. William knew that he had set the terms and, as a gentleman, had to live by the timeline...no matter what the cost. This gave Debbie free reign, in the days before he left and while he would be gone, to make William's life a living hell.

In the days prior to his departure, whenever William went to work or left the apartment for other various and sundry reasons, Debbie found numerous ways of showing her displeasure over the break up. She shattered every record album he owned, including the really old ones that may have been worth something; she ripped up all of his photographs, even the ones of he and Tilly together as children; she took his two bamboo fishing rods and snapped them in half, tossing the treasured gifts from his mother into an old remnant bin behind the tailor shop; she brought every piece of jewelry he owned, including the simple band of gold given to him by his mother that once belonged to his great grandmother, to a pawn shop and bought herself new clothes with the proceeds; and finally, Debbie took as many plates as she could carry from the kitchen cabinet and smashed them over a large rock that sat about twenty feet in from the main county road. When William heard about this last exploit, he dutifully drove over to the secluded spot covered in large shards of glass and picked up as many of the sharp pieces as he could, slicing his fingers to ribbons in the process.

William remained patient and even-tempered, though, amidst the various humiliations and indignities to which Debbie subjected him. There seemed to be nothing, absolutely nothing, that she could say or do to get his goat because he knew that soon, it would all be over; he would leave town to be with Tilly and Skeet and upon his return, she would be gone...permanently. He couldn't wait for that time to come because he would be rid of her—rid of the insults, the ridicule, and the long tirades. How he hated the long tirades. It was true enough that he was doing a slow burn on the inside because, after all, there was only so much a man could take. Outwardly, though, he remained ever the gentleman. That, above all else, angered Debbie all the more.

"Why do you let her treat you that way?" asked Mr. Pantaloni. "Mama mia!" he exclaimed, bringing his hand to his forehead. "You say nothing to make her stop! And talk about airing your dirty laundry out in public! Mrs. Pantaloni spent the better part of yesterday afternoon plucking your undershirts, long johns, and other articles of clothing out of the thorny bushes along the driveway. It took her all night to remove the thorns from her fingers. Mama mia!"

William suppressed a smile after picturing the scene that Mr. Pantaloni described. Poor Mrs. Pantaloni! The thought of his underwear in the bushes was tragically comical, but it was nothing to smile about. Debbie was really making a jackass out of him.

"I appreciate your concern, Mr. Pantaloni," William began, "and please apologize to Mrs. Pantaloni for me for all the trouble she went through to retrieve my clothing. I am thankful for that. I can assure you, though, that it will all be over soon...very soon."

That being said, William began to prepare for his trip and would meticulously tend to every detail. After Debbie had gone off to work, he gathered up whatever clothing hadn't been thrown out of the window and packed it all into an old suitcase along with his wallet, keys, and identification. He also cleaned out the fridge by eating the leftovers and tossing old condiment bottles and jars into the trash. William even scrambled the last egg and placed it in the pie tin on the tailor shop steps for Mr. Pantaloni's cat, Meatball. His careful attention to every trifle was exacting. He went on to cancel the evening newspaper and paid all of his outstanding bills, even giving Mr. Pantaloni two months rent in advance. Finally, William drew all of the shades in the apartment, washed the dirty dishes in the sink, and turned off the gas, which tended to leave a slight odor in the kitchen if the window wasn't periodically opened a crack. In the back of his mind, William thought that Debbie might move out of the apartment sooner rather than later if she saw that it had been basically cleaned out, devoid of the daily necessities. He hoped that the dark, empty shell would prompt her to pack her suitcases immediately and be gone, knowing that there was no longer anything left for which to stay.

William would leave his tidy apartment above the tailor shop to embark upon the noblest deed of his lifetime...of any man's lifetime. As for Debbie, he would never again give her or their disastrous relationship a second thought. William felt that she represented nothing more than a bad chapter in his life that was finally coming to its tragic end. This he would accept without reservation or disappointment. *Yes indeed*, he determined with a sense of gratification, *it will all be over soon...very soon.*

Chapter 16

Trying to Instigate Some Sort of Promise

When today fails to offer the justification for hope,
tomorrow becomes the only grail worth pursuing

— Arthur Miller, *Death of a Salesman*

William surmised that his first encounter with Skeet after having learned they were brothers would be painfully awkward. Yes, he had known Skeet all his life...as Tilly's boyfriend. This new revelation...bombshell really...would put a different spin on things. Would he really be able to face him without feeling odd, even embarrassed? Added to that was the frightful circumstance of Skeet's health. It was an overwhelming situation and William had plenty of time to think about it on the long drive to City Hospital.

He thought about other things too: his mother and how much he missed her, even though her last days were so difficult for him; Christine and her shameless flirtations which, to William, were both tantalizing and absurd; and finally, there was Debbie who would no longer be that looming aggravation, that thorn in his side who made his days increasingly miserable. William's head was awash with all of these entanglements, these bizarre threads that now embodied the fabric of his life that had suddenly been turned upside down by Tilly's revelation. Interestingly enough, though, he felt a surprising tranquility within himself. Above all else, he knew he was headed...in the right direction.

***

When William arrived at the hospital I was there to greet him, barely able to put my gratitude into words. We hugged... and cried.

"Are you ready for all of this?" I asked.

"I am, Tilly," William answered with confidence, "and I'm at total peace right now...with everything."

He smiled at me and took my hand.

"Everything is going to be okay, you know," William quietly reassured me, gently squeezing my hand.

"I know," I said, struggling to hold back my tears.

"Let's go take care of this thing," said my brother, kiddingly puffing out his chest, ready to fight the good and noble fight.

We walked down the long hospital corridor hand in hand. It felt wonderful to have William there for Skeet's sake...and for mine. Skeet had me to lean on, but now I had someone too.

First, I took William to meet Flanders Trumbull who would explain the entire procedure to my brother, focusing especially on his *role* in the process as a donor.

"So, you're Skeet's half brother," said Flanders who didn't know the *entire* story behind William's relationship to Skeet, a story far too fantastic to repeat to everyone even though Ma was dead and buried.

He knew enough, though.

"You're doing something wonderful for your brother," Flanders commented with sincere admiration as he perused

89

through the numerous papers on his clipboard.

William smiled weakly and said nothing, feeling a bit intimidated by the sheer gravity of it all.

"Barring any unforeseen circumstances and assuming right now that your human leukocyte antigens are a good match to your brother's," Flanders continued, "I'd say we can probably start harvesting your stem cells within the next few weeks. Of course, I'll have to check your genetic markers to make certain that you *are* a match."

I could tell that William was trying to keep up with everything Flanders was saying.

"If and when you find that I *am* a match, then what?" asked William.

"We'll give you a thorough physical right away and if everything checks out, I will then begin the process of taking cells from your pelvic bone," Flanders explained. "These are the cells most often used in a bone marrow transplant. Enough marrow must be harvested in order to collect a large number of healthy stem cells."

"Will this hurt?" William asked understandably.

"No, it won't" said Flanders. "You'll be given general anesthesia. Afterwards, you may feel sore for a few days."

"So, how will you get these cells out of my bone?" William questioned as though he were afraid to know the answer.

"I'll insert a large needle..." the doctor began.

"Why does everything always have to involve a large needle?" William interrupted skittishly.

"Large needles make things more fun," Flanders joked... but William was not amused.

The doctor cleared his throat and proceeded with his explanation.

"Anyway," Flanders continued seriously, "I'll insert a particular type of needle, used solely for this procedure, through your skin and into the back of your hipbone. I will then pull out the thick liquid marrow through that needle. This is repeated until enough marrow has been harvested."

William was fascinated as the doctor went on.

"The harvested marrow will be filtered, stored in a special solution, and then frozen. When I'm ready to give Skeet your marrow, the frozen solution will be thawed and given to him through a vein, just like a blood transfusion. Your cells will then travel to his bone marrow."

"Will he feel better right away?" William asked.

"Over time, your cells will hopefully engraft and begin to make new blood cells," said Flanders. "This will take anywhere from two to four weeks and should boost his chances for a full recovery. Please understand that there are no guarantees, but you're providing a greater chance...a greater hope," Flanders concluded.

"When may we begin?" asked William anxiously.

"I'll swab the inside of your cheek right now. If the genetic markers obtained from your cheek cells indicate that you *are* a match, then I'll start the ball rolling immediately," Flanders said as he patted William on the shoulder. "Be patient. We won't know for at least a week whether or not I can use you."

After Flanders swabbed the inside of his cheek and drew a vile of blood for good measure, William was finally ready to see Skeet.

"You'll have to wear a mask," I told him, "and I have to warn you...he doesn't look all that great right now. He's lost most of his hair and he's feeling tired and weak today. He can't wait for all of this to be over so that he can go home. That's all he dreams about...going home."

My eyes filled with tears again, but I was grateful that I could show such emotion in front of my brother. I certainly couldn't show it in front of Skeet.

"He'll go home soon," said William softly as he placed his arm around my shoulders. "We'll *all* be able to go home soon."

"How *are* things at your place?" I asked, quickly wiping my tears away with a tissue as William and I walked together, arm in arm, down the long hospital corridor toward Skeet's room.

"They're terrific *now*," said William. "Debbie should be all moved out by the time I get back."

"Thank goodness," I said with a sigh of relief. "She wasn't right for you, William...and she wasn't very nice...sorry to say."

I felt badly about having mentioned that, but William didn't seem to mind and he certainly didn't jump to Debbie's defense.

"I know she wasn't right for me," said William quietly, nodding his head in agreement. "Believe me, that's why she's out of my life...for good."

He seemed quite sure of that. As a matter of fact, I was impressed with William's overall confidence. He clearly wanted *me* to lean on *him*.

William and I dismissed any further discussion of Debbie as we approached Skeet's room. My brother braced himself and took in a deep breath. Throughout their lives, he and Skeet had talked a thousand times before as buddies. This time, they would talk as brothers.

When we walked into his room, Skeet was sound asleep. William was deeply moved upon seeing him so pale and drawn.

"He looks small in that bed," William commented in a whisper, "and vulnerable too."

"Vulnerable is the right word," interrupted Flanders Trumbull as he quickly breezed into the room to look at his patient. "We'll give him as many supportive therapies as possible to boost him up in preparation for the transplant. In the meantime, it's just a waiting game."

Flanders was quick in his examination of Skeet, not finding anything new or unexpected. He jotted down a few notes on his clipboard and briskly made his way toward the door, off no doubt to diagnose a strange malady or pluck some helpless soul away from a grave to which he had strayed too close. He was prolific in his successes and had the track record to prove it, but nailing him down for a conversation was like trying to trap lightning in a bottle. He was definitely a man who didn't like to linger unless he was flirting or lecturing. Once you had his attention, though, he was all yours.

***

William followed Flanders out into the hallway as he was leaving Skeet's room.

"What if I'm not a match?" he asked the doctor in a whisper that went straight to the point. "Will my brother die?"

As he glanced back into the room, William could see Tilly gently stroking Skeet's hair...and praying. Flanders put his hand on William's shoulder.

"If you're not a match, then I'll find someone else who is," Flanders reassured him. "Believe me, I will do everything in my power."

"Tilly says that you're pretty much a god around here and that if there's anyone who can pull Skeet through his illness, it's you," William commented, informing the doctor of his expectations in a backhanded sort of way.

Flanders quickly understood William's drift, but even more meaningful to him was the glowing praise bestowed upon him by a woman he could never have. He perked up immediately and concurred...whole-heartedly and immodestly.

"I would agree," said Flanders, "that if there is *anyone* who can pull Skeet through his illness, it's me."

His eyes were burning with a strong conviction, and William could sense his total self-possession.

"Then you're confident that my brother can lick this thing," said William, attempting to instigate some sort of promise that a smart doctor would never make...even if he *were* Flanders Trumbull.

"I *am* confident," said Flanders, "but I also say my prayers at night before going to bed."

William was taken aback.

"Really?" said William. "I thought that doctors like you relied solely upon medicine and scientific fact. Hell, I figured you to be a die-hard pragmatist."

"I *am* a man of science, but also a man of faith...and don't let that get around," Flanders said with a crooked smile. "There are no guarantees in this life, William, so relying upon a little divine intervention never hurts. It gives me the strength and confidence to push through those stubborn cases and get the job done, especially when I'm at a loss..."

Flanders caught himself and suddenly stopped short. Nonetheless, he had admitted enough, this man who fancied himself to be...above the rest.

"Like I said, I'll do everything in my power," Flanders brusquely reiterated. "That's all I can promise."

The two men looked at each other with a mutual understanding. William knew that Flanders Trumbull had nothing further to say, and it was time to go back into the room to be with Skeet anyway.

The two shook hands and parted as William immediately returned to his sister's side. They spoke in whispers as they watched Skeet sleep. William couldn't help but be a little nervous. After all, Skeet would awaken sooner or later and they would see each other for the first time...face to face...as brothers.

***

Skeet slowly opened his eyes to see William and me smiling down upon him. He returned a feeble smile, feeling a great sense of relief.

"I'm here, Skeet," William said softly, taking his hand. "I'm here."

At that moment, William knew that he had been wrong to think that his first encounter with Skeet, after having learned that they were related, would be an awkward one...it was anything but. And he also knew that, above all else, he was where he belonged...with his brother.

Chapter 17

The Waiting Game

Some rise by sin, and some by virtue fall.

—Shakespeare, *Measure for Measure*

The two brothers exchanged heartfelt words, but Skeet was too weak to stay awake for long. He quickly fell back into a comfortable and restful sleep, prompting Flan to encourage William and I to go back to my apartment for some relaxation of our own and a bite to eat. The test results were slow in coming, but the long wait gave William and me a chance to talk. We hadn't really spoken deeply and privately since our mother's death and so many things in our relationship had been left unsaid. Especially sketchy for me were William's growing up years. I knew him and adored him as a small child, but beyond that time my infrequent trips back home from college and then medical school were merely obligatory in nature...far too brief, really, to take serious notice of William's life with Ma, much less understand it...or even care to try.

"You were busy becoming a doctor," William said to me. "I understood that."

"I was so absorbed in my studies, in my own life, that your life just blew right by me. I wasn't always there for you when I should have been," I lamented. "I regret having been so consumed."

"You had no choice," William said consolingly in his usual, ever-understanding manner.

"I suppose not," I said, "but Ma slipped so far away from me that I couldn't do anything for her and, unfortunately, she took you right along with her into that abyss of demons. It wasn't that you didn't take excellent care of her, but at what cost to your own life?"

"Well, one positive thing that came out of it was that I couldn't rush off to marry Debbie," William said gratefully. "When I look back on it now, I think I used poor Ma's illness as an excuse so that I wouldn't *have* to marry her right away. It took Ma's death to finally make me realize that deep down inside I really didn't *want* to marry her at all. My heart just wasn't in it...and *that* was the only excuse I had left."

"At least you realized it and didn't make a terrible mistake," I said.

"Thank God for that," William commented quietly as he blankly stared at nothing in particular. "I definitely avoided a *tremendous* blunder."

William let out a long sigh.

"Well, I suppose I wish her luck," he said.

"Don't worry, you'll find someone to love, little brother," I said with a reassuring smile.

"Oh, I know that," William confirmed. "It won't be easy, though...finding the right girl. You were lucky, Tilly. You always knew that Skeet was the one for you right from the start, even back when you were kids! Now, that's a beautiful thing."

I smiled as I thought back to my childhood. Whenever I thought about Skeet and me as kids, I lovingly thought of Ma too.

"I always wished that Ma would eventually find someone to love," I repined. "She certainly had her share of suitors, but none of her relationships ever seemed to work out. She always stopped short of allowing herself to love any man after Pa died."

As I sucked ice water with lemon through a straw, William slowly sipped on a hot cup of tea made in Ma's old kettle. He had been listening intently to what I had to say, visibly bristling at my comments about Ma's relationships. I thought that to be odd at first, but then simply chalked it up to a probable discomfort that men must feel whenever there is discussion of their mother's love life. Or so I thought...

"Well, with the exception of *one* man," William interjected, shaking his head.

"Excuse me?" I said in total surprise. "I never knew any of this! Whom exactly are you talking about?"

"Do you remember the Reverend Chauncey from the little white church?" William asked, placing his teacup on the table.

"Sure I do," I said immediately. "He was quite a character. I remember that when I was a kid he was once sweet on Ma, but it never went any further than that...*or did it?*"

My eyes went wide with an irrepressible curiosity but I also felt, at the same time, like we were inexcusably engaging in shameless back room gossip about our own mother. William took in a deep breath and exhaled loudly. He clasped his hands behind his head and rocked back in his chair.

"Well, Ma swore me to secrecy, but I suppose there isn't any harm in telling you now," he said.

"In telling me what?" I asked.

"It's just that she didn't want to worry you," William said.

"Worry me about what?" I asked impatiently.

"You see, back around the time when you were in medical school, Ma married the reverend for, what turned out to be, a very short while," William specified, breaking the news to me as gently as possible.

My jaw dropped as I situated myself on the large, lumpy sofa in the living room, ready to hear all about the entire sordid affair. I was flabbergasted to say the least. Ma was always an expert at keeping secrets, but this one blindsided me. What next?

"Start at the beginning and don't leave anything out," I warned him.

William began his story as though he were entertaining small children sitting on the floor of a kindergarten classroom...legs crossed, faces cradled in little hands...waiting to hear something magical and fascinating. I anticipated a juicy, wicked tale and I wasn't disappointed.

"Well, you know how shady the reverend always was," William began, "collecting his nickels and dimes from the poor folks of the county who hung onto his every word. Of course, these needy souls always assumed that their money was going directly toward the upkeep of the little white church."

"Even as kids, Skeet and I knew that he was pocketing the money he collected!" I interjected quickly, suddenly recalling just how much I disliked the reverend back then... and what a phony man he was!

"Well, you were right," William continued. "He was, and still is, a phony man. After a while, his deceptive ways caught up to him. The good people who unwittingly subsidized the extravagant lifestyle of this crooked rake began to wonder why the church roof wasn't being repaired as promised, the broken windows replaced, or the dilapidated pews sanded down and oiled once again; invariably, at least one person a Sunday came out of the morning service complaining of a sliver in his backside."

"It sounds like the little white church fell into total disrepair," I commented. "What a shame."

"Oh, it did," William concurred, "forcing the county faithful to attend services over in Leather Junction. Reverend Chauncey was distraught, claiming to have lost his flock. What he really lost, however, was his gravy train. Basically, the church collapsed and the reverend found himself out in the cold.

"Is this where Ma came in?" I asked, my eyes widening again.

"Yes, this is *exactly* where Ma came in," William confirmed, "and bailed the fat bastard out of his troubles. She paid to have the roof repaired and the broken windows replaced. She went into the church herself and, along with a handful of other lady volunteers, sanded down the pews and polished them with lemon oil, bringing them back to their former gloss. The building was opened for business once again and the reverend couldn't be happier as the county faithful made their way back to the little white church."

I continued to listen to my brother's astonishing story as my mouth opened a bit wider with every tantalizing word.

"Now mind you," William continued, "I was certain that Ma made her monumental gesture for the love of God and not for the love of the reverend. But, of course, he misconstrued the importance that she attached to her church as some sort of grab for his affection. He began to court her..."

"He courted her again?" I blurted out, averse to the thought.

"...and within a short amount of time they were serious," William resumed after my interruption, not skipping a beat. "I didn't like the man, but Ma felt that as a boy of thirteen, I needed some sort of male influence in my life. I suppose that wasn't such a bad idea at the time, given the fact that I only ever had Ma, but her choice for a husband..."

William stopped short, shaking his head.

"I can't believe he got back into her good graces," I mused. "He wanted to marry her before you were even born, but she wouldn't hear of it. I guess she figured she was doing something good for your sake," I determined.

"Yes, I believe that's what she thought," William agreed, "and for a short time, things went along quite well. The reverend took me fishing, helped me with my homework, and was there at the dinner table every night to compliment Ma's cooking. He even helped out with the chores around the house."

"Where did it all go wrong?" I asked.

"He became an abusive man, Tilly," William said with contempt, shaking his head again. "He would drink way too much and then stumble around the house, breaking lamps and yelling at Ma. She also caught him in a pack of lies concerning his whereabouts on several different occasions."

"Where was he *really*?" I asked curiously.

"Ma somehow found out that he was actually playing around with one of the ladies who had volunteered to clean up the little white church," William said, recalling what our mother had unearthed about her husband.

"That must have been the last straw for Ma," I said confidently, thinking that she would have never tolerated a cheating husband.

"Not quite," said my brother. "The last straw for Ma was when the reverend and I got into a heated argument that spiraled out of control."

"What do you mean *out of control*?" I asked, almost afraid to know the answer.

"One day," William began as he clasped his hands together and sat on the edge of his chair, "the reverend went on a drinking binge and began to treat Ma poorly. He was yelling, throwing things and, at one point, even grabbed her arm and wrenched it."

As my brother spoke, I could feel the anger rising inside of me.

"Of course, I didn't like what was going on one bit," William said as he shifted in his seat, his voice slightly cracking with emotion.

He suddenly turned pensive before continuing as he recalled that awful day in his childhood. I didn't say a word.

"The reverend left the house after calling Ma a string of nasty names and drove off toward the little white church. I followed on foot with the intention of defending Ma's honor. At first, I ran after the car as it swerved from one side of the road to the other, keeping a pretty good pace too, until I eventually peeled off into the woods, running as fast as I could until I reached the church. The reverend's car was parked outside at a crooked angle and the driver's side door was still wide open," William recalled.

My brother took another sip of his tea before continuing.

I was frozen, unable to move a muscle.

"After catching my breath, I went inside," he said. "The church was dimly lit, but I could hear a voice calling out to me from one of the pews. *Looking for me, boy?* slurred the Reverend Chauncey. His voice echoed throughout the church as the smell of lemon oil permeated the air. I turned to see him sprawled out on one of the pews in a drunken stupor."

"What did you do then?" I asked, completely captivated by the story.

William could sense my enthrallment. He continued to clearly recall the long ago drama as though it had happened only yesterday.

"Well, I went over to him and grabbed him by the collar, tugging on it hard until he rolled off the pew and onto the floor," William remembered. "I kicked him a couple of times, but he suddenly had me by the ankle and twisted it violently, pulling me down onto the floor with him. We grappled for several minutes during which time I landed a few good punches, but eventually he was able to yank me by the hair and repeatedly pound my head against the cold stone floor of the church. I was in excruciating pain and began to feel faint but before I could pass out, someone had unexpectedly broken the reverend's grip on me. Within seconds, I was completely out of his reach after having been dragged by my feet out of harm's way. I looked up to see Ma kicking the intoxicated reverend repeatedly as he tried to shield his face with his hands. She then stood back, breathless and in a furious rage. Without stopping to think about it, Ma threatened his life. *If you ever lay a finger on my son again, I'll kill you,* Ma spat down upon the reverend. She gave him one more kick for good measure, picked me up off the floor, and took me home."

"Then what happened?" I asked, thoroughly stunned by my brother's story. "What did Ma do next?"

"After we got home, she put me to bed and marched straight to the County Courthouse where she filed for a divorce that very same day," William recollected with a slight smile. "That's when I knew just how strong of a woman she was in both body and spirit. She was my fierce protector, Tilly, and I believe to this day that if the reverend had ever laid another finger on me, she would have followed through on her threat and killed him on the spot. From that day forward, I swore that I would always protect and take care of Ma when the time came that she needed me."

William nodded his head as he strummed his fingers nervously on the coffee table.

"Yes, she was one strong woman," he kept repeating as he stood up from his chair and walked over to the window, staring blankly into the darkness.

I could still see his head nodding ever so slightly.

My mouth agape I couldn't speak, as the words seemed to stick in my throat. Anyhow, what words could possibly express what I was feeling? All I could get out was *wow* and *that's unbelievable.* I was always in awe of Ma's strength and utter resolve; William's story only served to confirm what I already knew. Not to mention the fact that she had already killed a man in retaliation for what he had done to her. I had no doubt in my mind that she would have killed again in defense of her son. Poor Ma. The incident between William and the Reverend Chauncey was just another sordid episode in the twisted and violent life of that ill-fated woman. There is no wonder why she went completely crazy.

William had both of his hands stuffed into the front pockets of his jeans. One hand jiggled the coins in the left pocket while the other played with the keys in the right. He appeared to be ill at ease as he moved away from the window and began to pace, the story he had just told me apparently dredging up a traumatic and painful memory. That was what I thought...until he turned to me gravely.

"She did it, didn't she?" William asked in a low, barely audible voice. "It was Ma who murdered Sheffield LeMay. It dawned on me...as I recalled that story."

I froze as William continued as though he were in a hypnotic trance.

"Knowing her...knowing how fierce she was...and the blood...the blood that she always claimed to be dripping from her hands. It was his blood, wasn't it? My mother killed my father...and you knew it all along."

I began to tremble all over. This was, yet again, another conversation that I did not want to have with my brother. William was, however, the undeniable apex of Ma's regrettable past, the constant reminder that her life had been chillingly adulterated forever. I always feared that one day he would put two and two together, thus uncovering the entire dirty mess for himself. It appeared that William's day of reckoning had arrived.

"William," I began gingerly, only to be interrupted by the ringing of the telephone. We both jumped and I ran to answer it, the thought of Skeet never at all far from my mind.

"Yes, Flan...I understand," I said with a smile, giving William a thumb's up after noticing his concerned expression. "We'll be there soon."

I hung up the telephone and breathed a sigh of relief. William looked at me, all thoughts of the past now pushed to the back of his mind.

"What is it, Tilly...good news?" asked my brother.

"We have to get back to the hospital," I said with elated urgency. "You're a match."

Chapter 18

Foul Play

By the pricking of my thumbs, something wicked this way comes.

—Shakespeare, *Macbeth*

At first, the short ride to the hospital was silent. William was pensive, almost sullen.

"William, just how important is it for you to know who murdered Sheffield LeMay all those years ago?" I asked.

"Important enough...if my mother was the murderer," he answered in an edgy tone of voice.

"Please don't be angry, William," I pleaded quietly. "Ma is dead and so is Sheffield LeMay. It makes no sense to dig up the past, especially when it has no bearing on the future...and that's where we all need to set our sights right now...on the future. Let the dead rest, William. They can't hurt each other any longer...nor us, for that matter."

William listened intently to what I had to say and then bowed his head in contemplation. Looking out of the passenger window of my car, he silently watched other vehicles and passers by with a deliberate eye as though he were expecting to see someone he knew.

"So many people...each with his own story," William said with a smirk as he shook his head. "Do you think that anyone out there could possibly have a life story as murky as mine?"

His question was a rhetorical one.

"Do you really *care*?" I asked pointedly. "Is what happened all those years ago enough to jade everything you loved about Ma, enough to alter your self-respect and the integrity with which you've always lived your life, enough to distort your outlook on your own *future*? C'mon, William... think about it," I encouraged him. "Look at what you're about to do for Skeet. Your unselfish gesture gives us all hope for a brighter future...his, yours, and our future together...as a family. Don't hang yourself up on the past," I warned him. "That will only drag you into dark places. Stay in the light, William, and live for today...and for the future."

I felt I had made my case eloquently and I think William felt so too.

"I suppose you're right," he sighed. "As a matter of fact, I *know* you're right."

His mood brightened considerably, enabling me to breathe a little easier.

"Let's go see Skeet," I said with a smile.

William smiled back and squeezed my hand before he got out of the car. It was time for us to move ahead into the future...as a family.

Flanders Trumbull greeted us in the main corridor of the third floor where we talked as we slowly strolled toward Skeet's room.

"Well, I trust that the two of you had a sufficient rest at home these last couple of hours before coming back to the hospital," Flanders said. "You'll both need to give Skeet all the strength and support you can channel. Once the transplant occurs, he can expect an around the clock barrage of bad symptoms, all short term of course, but nonetheless difficult."

Flanders' voice trailed off a bit as he studied each paper on his ever-present clipboard.

"He'll not only feel poorly, but he'll be at his most vulnerable," the doctor continued. "A low blood cell count, fatigue, nausea, vomiting, and hair loss," he listed off, "are just some of the side effects he may experience."

The three of us continued to walk slowly down the long corridor, stepping into a small alcove across from Skeet's room. William was grave, although I had already known what to expect.

"He'll be so sick," my brother lamented, looking back and forth between Flan and me.

"It is at *that* point," Flanders reassured William, "that I and the rest of his medical team will heighten our vigilance of his overall health."

"Flan, what exactly will you do to safeguard Skeet's health at that time," I asked, placing my hand on William's shoulder. "I know that there are many supportive therapies..."

"Yes, there are," the good doctor quietly interrupted. "I'll give him drugs to keep his immune system in check and over the next few weeks that follow, his blood will be tested regularly to make sure that cell replacement is progressing correctly. Additionally, he may require antibiotics, red blood cell or platelet transfusions, and meticulous guidance of his nutritional intake."

"It sounds as though you'll be watching him closely," William said, feeling a modicum of relief.

"Like a mother hen, twenty-four hours a day, seven days

a week...I promise," said Flanders.

"We should see positive results within a couple of weeks, shouldn't we, Flan?" I asked optimistically.

"Usually, within a couple of weeks after the transplanted stem cells have been infused, they will begin to make new white blood cells, followed by new platelets and, several weeks later, by new red blood cells," said Flanders.

"When will he be able to come home?" asked William as he took my hand.

"He'll need to stay here until his blood count rises to a safe level," Flanders said definitively. "I will have to exercise great prudence in that regard. The last thing you would want me to do is jump the gun by sending him home too early...*believe* me."

Flanders seemed to be pleading his case to William, but I wasn't at all surprised by his response. It was best to err on the side of caution anyway, something I had naturally come to expect from Flan.

"Once his counts rise to my satisfaction, though, I'll be able to discharge him and he'll be seen in the outpatient clinic for several weeks for additional therapies and possible platelet transfusions."

"That doesn't sound *too* bad," said William as he choked up.

"It's a long road," I whispered to my brother.

"Under the *best* of circumstances," Flanders quickly reminded me with a cautionary finger. "That timeline can be sabotaged at any given point by infection or other types of complications, but that is why I'm here...to provide Skeet with all of the medical support that is within my power to deliver. And you two will be his cheerleaders."

Flanders took William by the arm.

"Please don't think that I'm minimizing your role in all of this," he said. "You are giving Skeet something that I can't. That makes you the most important person, the linchpin so to speak, of this entire operation and an indispensable member of your brother's medical team. Generally, my ego would prevent me from commending anyone other than myself for my patients' recoveries," Flanders said kiddingly in a not-so-confidential whisper, "but in cases such as this," he said, turning serious again, "it is the stem cell donor who has my utmost respect, appreciation and well-deserved credit."

He shook William's hand heartily. I smiled at my brother, laying my head on his shoulder. Our emotions were so raw, so appreciable.

"Please understand further that if for some reason the transplant does not work," Flanders said to William in all sincerity, "you are not to consider yourself at fault, and the magnanimity of your gesture will remain intact. You, William, are the hero here," Flan concluded, patting my brother on the back.

This was a side of Flan that I had never seen before and I liked it. He was rarely humble, making this kind gesture toward William all the more extraordinary.

"Now, go see Skeet," he said. "I have rounds to finish and then I'll be in to talk to the three of you. I intend for the transplant to take place soon...very soon."

Flan left us to tend to his other patients, moving like a knight, off to save someone else from a misfortunate medical situation. I found myself in awe of the man like everyone else, hanging all of my hopes squarely on his shoulders.

The next day, after a thorough physical and a frank discussion that determined his mental and emotional state, William successfully cleared the last hurdle, earning Flan's long-awaited *final* approval to be Skeet's donor. That same evening, he underwent general anesthesia and sacrificed three bags of healthy stem cells for the sake of his brother. Afterward, as he lay in his hospital bed feeling a vague discomfort from the long needle that had been inserted into his hip during the procedure, William also felt great satisfaction and a strong pride. He had never before been given the opportunity to make so noble a gesture, and surely would never encounter such a chance again...not on this scale...not in this lifetime. William closed his eyes, relishing a feeling of deep peace.

Suddenly, a knock on his hospital room door caused William to swim up from near sleep. *It must be Tilly or Dr. Trumbull*, he thought, smiling contentedly without opening his eyes.

"Mr. Figlit?" came the strange voice from the doorway.

William promptly opened his eyes in response to the unfamiliar voice that belonged to neither his sister nor Flanders Trumbull, startled to see two county police officers standing in front of his bed.

"We apologize for bothering you at this time, sir," said one of the officers, "but do you know a Miss Deborah Mead?"

William would slur his words a bit, but he was fully cognizant of the question...and their uninvited presence.

"Yes I do," William said, feeling slightly foggy. "She was my girlfriend, but we broke it off about two weeks ago. Why?"

"Well, we're sorry to have to tell you this, sir, but we believe that she may have been a victim of...foul play.

Chapter 19

Inextricably Embroiled

We cast a shadow on something wherever we stand,
and it is no good moving from place to place to save things;
because the shadow always follows."

—E.M. Forster, *A Room With a View*

"What do you mean...foul play?" asked a confused William, not really comprehending the officer's statement.

He still felt clouded over, his grasp of what had just been told to him thin at best. Feelings of contentment and deep peace were suddenly gone as his mood quickly sobered. By forcing himself into a heightened awareness of his surroundings, William had come back to reality, abandoning his dreamlike serenity. He could not deny that he was now alarmed as he began to tremble a bit.

"What's going on here?" asked Flanders Trumbull as he swooped in on the officers like an eagle guarding its nest. "This man is my patient," he said. "Who gave you permission to speak to him?"

"No, no...it's okay," said William, waving his hand. "The officers were just telling me something about my former girl-friend, something about...*foul play.*"

William struggled to sit up as the words stuck in his throat, his face revealing disbelief.

"You say you broke it off about two weeks ago?" asked the officer.

"Yes, that's right," said William.

"Was it an amicable breakup?" asked the other officer.

"No, not really," said William, telling the truth. "She did some spiteful things after I told her she needed to move out."

William was beginning to feel aggravated because once again, Debbie was making his life miserable and they weren't even together anymore...or even in the same town!

"What types of spiteful things?" asked one of the officers.

"Oh, you know, mostly petty things...breaking dishes, throwing my clothes out of the bedroom window...and the like," William trailed off, remembering the beloved bamboo fishing rods from his mother that had been purposely snapped in half and discarded.

"Did she recently pawn your jewelry, Mr. Figlit?" asked the same officer.

"Why, yes she did," answered William, surprised that the police knew about that.

William began to realize the implications of the officers' questioning and the gravity of the situation in which he seemed to be inextricably embroiled. Apparently, it didn't matter that he was lying in a hospital bed after having done something incredibly selfless for a brother he didn't even know he had; it appeared that he was under investigation just the same.

"What's going on?" asked William impatiently. "What has happened to Debbie?"

"We don't know yet," answered one of the officers. "We were hoping that you could tell us. About a week ago, we received a phone call from an alarmed man, one Analdi Pantaloni, complaining of loud fighting in the apartment above his tailor shop. He claimed to have heard yelling,

114

items being thrown, and objects being broken. When we arrived, Mr. Pantaloni told us that the noise had stopped, but he gave us your name and that of your girlfriend as the two occupants of said apartment. We walked upstairs expecting to speak with the two of you, but the place was empty."

"Well, then who was fighting up there?" asked William.

"Was it you and Deborah Mead, Mr. Figlit?" one of the officers asked.

"Certainly not," said William in an offended tone. "Mr. Pantaloni can vouch for me. He knew that I had plans to leave the apartment to be with my sister and her fiancé."

"Yes, but he claimed that he didn't know exactly *when* you were leaving or if, in fact, you had even left yet at all," said one of the officers.

"And his understanding of *where* you were actually going or *when* you'd be back was vague," chimed in the other. "It seemed as though the more we questioned him, the more confused he got concerning your whereabouts at the time of his phone call."

"Well, I obviously wasn't there when you arrived, gentlemen," said William, clearly annoyed, "so how could you possibly think that I was involved in this so-called fight? And what's all this talk about foul play?" he asked, now wide-awake and perfectly alert. "If the apartment was empty when you got up there, why then do you think that Debbie was a victim of *foul play*?"

"When we entered the apartment," began one officer, "it wreaked of gas. The four burners on the stove were all turned on, but not lit. Luckily, there wasn't enough of a gas build up to cause an explosion. We quickly turned the burners off and opened several windows to air the place out."

"I shut the gas off at the main valve before I left the apartment to come here," William contended.

"Well, someone deliberately turned it back on with the intention of blowing the apartment sky high," said one of the officers, "perhaps to cover up what we found next."

"What was that?" asked William, finding it hard to believe what he was hearing.

"We encountered a mess of broken furniture, shattered bric-a-brac, and blood...drops of blood everywhere. In the bathroom there was blood on the floor and in the sink. Additionally, the initials WF...your initials, sir...were smeared in blood on the bathroom mirror."

"I know nothing of *any* of this," William asserted. "When I left my apartment a week ago, it was immaculately clean. Debbie wasn't even *there*," he said, looking at each of the officers with a shocked expression.

Not even acknowledging what William had just said, the two men continued.

"After we left the bathroom and navigated our way through the broken plates and cups on the kitchen floor, we followed a path of blood drops down the back stairs and outside into the driveway," said one officer.

"And that was where the blood abruptly ended," said the other.

"So, what are you telling me?" asked William. "That she vanished into thin air?"

"No, sir," an officer corrected him. "We think that she was forced into her car and driven away."

"What makes you think that?" asked William.

"We found your girlfriend's abandoned car..." began one of the officers.

"*Ex*-girlfriend," William interrupted, now feeling absolutely irritated.

"We found *Miss Deborah Mead's* abandoned car," the officer begrudgingly corrected himself, "off the main county road on the outskirts of town. There was blood inside the car and a bloody pocketknife in one of the visors. Also, a work shirt with your name stitched above the front pocket was found stuffed under the driver's seat."

"Let me guess," William said sarcastically, "my shirt had blood on it too."

"That is correct," said the officer, now squinting at William with suspicious eyes, "and it is there in that abandoned car where our trail of evidence goes cold."

"The girl's parents haven't seen her in quite a while and no one around town has seen her either," said the other officer. "The department has initiated an extensive search of the woods off the main county road, but that's a lot of territory to cover."

William lay in his bed, listening silently. It all seemed so...fantastic.

"Can you help us in any way with this investigation, Mr. Figlit?" asked the officer who was still squinting at William with suspicious eyes.

His tone was stern and he acted as though he were fed up.

"No, I...I can't," stuttered William, raising his eyebrows and shaking his head.

"Are you sure?" asked the pushy officer.

"Yes, I'm sure," said William, decisively going on the offensive. "Damn sure."

"Then can you tell us why your fingers appear to have

been cut up?" the officer asked skeptically.

William picked up his hands and studied his fingers. He remembered how they stung and bled all the way home from the main county road after he had picked up the large shards of glass around the rock where Debbie had smashed the plates. Did those scars still show? Did he clean up all the blood that had stained the inside of his car? His thoughts churned in a mad frenzy. Admittedly, he had the appearance of someone suspect of a crime. Now what?

"This all sounds very interesting," interrupted Flanders Trumbull who had melted himself into a far corner of the room as he listened to the unexpected and bizarre exchange, "but my patient needs to rest now. You may speak to him later...*after* you've gotten my permission," he said pointedly. "I can assure you that he is not going anywhere."

The doctor immediately began to take William's blood pressure and pulse as the officers exchanged glances.

"I suppose that would be okay," said one of the men as he stared intently at William. "Please know that we would like to take a look at the inside of your vehicle."

"I assume you'll have a warrant," said William off-handedly.

"Do we need one?" the other officer asked flippantly.

William didn't like his tone of voice and decided not to respond.

As he lay in his bed in stony silence, William was afraid to move, afraid to utter one more word for fear it would incriminate him. He stared at the two officers and waited for them to speak their last and leave the room. He didn't have to wait long before they began to stroll slowly toward the door.

"Oh, and by the way," said one of the officers looking over his shoulder, "when we return, maybe you'll be able to enlighten us as to who may have stolen Mr. Pantaloni's car on the day he heard the loud fighting coming from your apartment."

William wanted to adamantly deny any knowledge of this, but he simply closed his eyes and gently shook his head from side to side.

"You rest now," said the officer, pausing at the door before walking out into the hospital corridor. "We'll be talking to you again soon...real soon."

Chapter 20

Polar Opposite Aspects

Life is to be lived, not controlled; and humanity is won by continuing to play in face of certain defeat.

—Ralph Ellison, *Invisible Man*

Several days passed quietly for both Skeet and William until life gave way at the critical juncture each man would face. Skeet began to receive William's bone marrow cells while William awaited word of Debbie's whereabouts. For his part, Flanders Trumbull kept a close watch on both men. The last thing the good doctor wanted was for William's legal predicament to have a deleterious effect on either Skeet *or* me. As it was, Skeet got sicker and sicker as the week progressed. He could hardly pick his head up off the pillow for the extreme fatigue that had swiftly assaulted his body.

"Par for the course," Flanders assured me. "Things are going exactly as they should. Everything is normal...quite normal."

Keeping that in mind, William and I gave Skeet the continual encouragement he needed to fight the good fight. His hair had noticeably thinned and it became difficult for him to eat, given the painful sores that now lined his mouth. And then there was the nausea...the acute nausea. Flanders gave him drugs for that, along with antibiotics and his first post-transplant transfusion.

"According to your blood test, the process of cell replacement is progressing as it should. We need more time, though, before we know whether or not the transplant is going to stick. You have a ways to go."

"*A ways to go...a ways to go...a ways to go,*" Skeet mumbled over and over again under his breath. He hated the phrase and he was sick of hearing it.

"You need to try and eat," I said. "It's important."

"I'm sick of jello," Skeet said with disgust.

"How about some broth," I suggested with a smile in an attempt to keep his spirits up.

"How about a steak...or a pizza...or a burger," Skeet spat out in frustration, his voice quivering slightly with emotion.

"I know it's difficult, darling," I said, stroking his thinning hair. "I know it's difficult."

Skeet's days consisted of lying in bed, getting up when he could, having his blood drawn for monitoring, and then... having his blood drawn for more monitoring. He was tired of having to wear a mask and seeing everyone else have to wear one too. It had been far too many days since he and I had kissed without the masks. How dreadful...and wearisome.

My brother, on the other hand, was experiencing his own trials. Figuring he had nothing to hide, William allowed the police to look at the inside of his car even though they had yet to apply for a warrant. After all, what could they possibly find except...

"There were several spatters of blood in your vehicle," reported one officer. "Three on the dashboard and one on the steering wheel. My partner is off to see the judge for a warrant right now."

"What for?" asked William in a cocky tone of voice. "I told

you I had *nothing* to hide. That's *my* blood in the car. I sliced my fingers while picking up shards of glass from the plates my girlfriend had smashed in the woods."

"Are you sure it isn't...her blood?" asked one of the officers.

"Damn sure," William said confidently.

"That's easy enough to check out, son," said one officer in a kindly tone of voice, obviously trying to coax a confession out of William.

"Go right ahead," my brother dared him.

"If the blood in your car matches any of the blood found in the apartment or in the abandoned car," the officer started to declare, "then you have a problem."

"I can assure you that it *will...not...match,*" William said pointedly, punctuating his words boldly with a challenging finger in the officer's face.

And so it went. Just as William had asserted over and over again, the police soon discovered that he had been telling the truth all along. The blood found in his car was indeed his and his alone while the blood found in the apartment and in the abandoned car matched Debbie's blood type exclusively, this determined by birth records obtained from her mother. The police could no longer contend that Debbie's blood was in William's car, or that William's blood was in the apartment or abandoned car, placing them back at square one. Of course, this could not definitively exonerate William for he would remain a person of interest...high interest. Who else would want to kill Deborah Mead? He hesitated to tell the police just how caustic a woman she was or just how miserable he felt when he was with her for fear that they would regard this as motive enough for him to kill her. They couldn't know just how desperately he wanted to be...*rid* of her.

William had planned on staying with me for a while anyway, but the police told him not to go too far just the same. That was okay with him as he and I were together to watch Skeet's health improve exponentially as the days passed. The sores in his mouth eventually disappeared, allowing him to enjoy a greater variety of foods. His hair thickened up a bit and the nausea disappeared altogether. He enjoyed taking walks with me down the long hospital corridors and he especially liked to visit other patients. It always gave him a special boost to hear someone say how wonderful he looked. Of course, he still had to wear a mask, but even that couldn't hide the fact that with each compliment he received, his smile got a little bit bigger. The best news of all was that his marrow was producing new white blood cells.

"So far, so good," said Flanders Trumbull. "Keep your chin up. I expect that your body will continue to make healthy white cells, followed by platelets and then red cells. Once your count goes up to that safe level," said Flanders, holding his hand up high in the air palm side down, "then you can go home."

"When will that be?" asked a tired, but grateful Skeet.

"Barring infection or some other complication, I'd say... maybe...three weeks," hedged the doctor, wrinkling his face.

"That long?" Skeet asked.

He was absolutely crestfallen.

"I won't release you unless I can be sure that your immune system will tolerate your being on the outside again," said Flanders. "Be patient. You are progressing nicely." And with that, the good doctor breezed out of the room as only *he* could, looking every bit the knight in shining armor.

Besides his therapeutic walks with me, Skeet enjoyed playing chess with the patient in the room next door to his. This was another saving grace as it remedied the boredom and alleviated the tedium of most days. When his almost daily blood draw had become the highlight of his routine, Skeet knew he had to find something else to do...something enjoyable, but not overtaxing. When Flanders gave him permission to play chess with Dunnith Nelligan, a willful stripling who was fighting his *own* cancer battle, Skeet jumped at the opportunity.

"Provided you both wear gloves and masks," Flanders reminded him.

For Skeet, daily life at the hospital had suddenly gone from humdrum to enjoyably tolerable. He looked forward to his chess games with Dunnith because the teenager was feisty, determined, and had all the makings of a survivor. Skeet, for his part, could always come up with a funny joke that would make his friend laugh until the tears fell. The two companions complimented and supported each other nicely, but there was no doubt about it—Dunnith was a pistol...a real character.

Dunnith Thomas Patrick Nelligan was born in the tiny fishing village of Killeen on Mulster, a most remote and private enclave of old salts that were devoted to their life on the Irish Sea. When the fish stopped biting, though, the Nelligans were obliged to gather up their meager belongings, secure passage on a boat bound for America and leave their beloved Ireland, Dunnith in tow. The boy loved his new and carefree life on the farmlands of America...until he got sick.

Now a young man of seventeen, he found himself fighting for his life and fight he did...with all the tenacity he could muster.

To that end, there wasn't a doctor spared his sarcastic quips or a nurse invulnerable to his boyish charms...given his knack for enchanting the ladies. Skeet continuously marveled at this sickly young man who could hold anyone he met in the palm of his hand with a smile most infectious and an irresistible manner. He was also clever and whimsical when it came to getting what he wanted. There was the time he glued together over two hundred tongue depressors, swiped shamelessly from a hospital supply closet, in the shape of a tree because he couldn't have a plant in his room. Then there was the time he molded an igloo out of mashed potatoes, corn and carrots, stuck a thermometer through the top and left it at the nurse's station because he felt his room was too cold.

The day the nurses found Dunnith pitching pennies into his bedpan, he was slumped over and weak. They put him back to bed and the young man languished for five days, no longer able to play chess with Skeet, charm the ladies, or revel in his boyish antics. When the family priest finally appeared to sprinkle holy water and give the last rights, everyone knew it was all but over for Dunnith Nelligan.

Skeet took to his bed, too upset to bid his chess partner a fond farewell or say thank you to the charismatic Irish lad who had managed to brighten everyone's day in a place that tended to be morbid and spiritless. And, of course, the inevitable question came to his mind—am I going to die too?

William and I did our level best to bolster Skeet's spirits after Dunnith Nelligan's passing. The rambunctious lad had come into his life, stayed for a short while and then departed all too soon, leaving Skeet and everyone else who knew him pained by his death, including Flanders Trumbull. The good doctor couldn't help but feel that Dunnith's death was *his* failure, a most uncommon happenstance in his storied career, and he withdrew into an impenetrable depression for a few days...something he had never experienced before. This was his first loss and for him it was a bitter experience. He made himself scarce until he could reconcile his feelings, often sitting for hours on end in the small hospital chapel. When he emerged two days later, Flanders was humble and a little bit frightened, but he was as determined as ever to pull Skeet through *his* health crisis. Doctor Jesus had finally come down to earth.

As for Skeet, he grieved for himself as well as for Dunnith.

"I'm a better person for having known Dunnith Nelligan," he commented to me, "but I have a deep pit in my gut right now—a deep, dark pit that I fear will swallow me up and send me to my maker too."

He had a far off look in his eye as he slowly shook his head. His fear was understandable...and normal.

"He was too young to die," Skeet lamented, "far too young."

In the meantime, fate had thrown an absurdly bizarre twist into the life of the magnanimous younger brother who had suddenly found himself suspect of foul play. William could not reconcile these polar opposite aspects of his life... the one that mirrored his unselfishness toward a brother he never knew he had, and the other in which he was mired in a dark pit of criminal suspicion...yet they existed, causing his head to spin uncontrollably in contrary directions. He was simply confounded by it all.

Despite his predicament, William felt quite safe and comfortable staying with me while giving Skeet all of the emotional support he could muster under the circumstances. He did admit, though, that he now found himself wondering from time to time *just how* everything would actually play out for Skeet, given the fact that Dunnith Nelligan's death had made him a little cynical about his brother's chances for a full recovery...or at least mindful that there are no guarantees in this life. And what of Debbie? Would the police ever find out what happened to her?

William's questions about Debbie would be answered sooner rather than later because only one week after Dunnith Nelligan's death did two County police officers come knocking on my apartment door.

"Is Mr. Figlit at home?" asked one of the officers after I opened the door.

"Here I am," said William, stepping out of the shadows of the small kitchen off of the living room. "What is it?"

He was sick to his stomach, afraid of what they were about to say.

"Sir, we are here to tell you that...we have found your girlfriend."

Chapter 21

Where We Can Be Together

Basically, at the very bottom of life, which seduces us all, there is only absurdity, and more absurdity. And maybe that's what gives us our joy for living, because the only thing that can defeat absurdity is lucidity.

— Albert Camus

"Is she dead?" William asked apprehensively, feeling as though he would faint.

"No, sir," one of the police officers immediately answered, "quite the contrary. We found her to be very much alive."

"Is she all right?" William asked, still feeling uneasy, but also a bit puzzled.

"May we come in, sir?" asked the other officer politely. "We would like to explain the entire situation to you and it is going to take a few minutes."

"It sounds like there is a story here," William said with a furrowed brow as he escorted the two officers into the living room.

"There is," answered one of the officers with a slight smile.

"May I offer the two of you a cup of coffee?" I asked.

"No, ma'am," both officers chimed in at the same time. "We need to say our piece and then get back to the County Police Department where both Deborah Mead and her niece Christine are sitting in a jail cell."

"What?" William said, his eyes wide with disbelief. "What

is going on here? All this time I thought that *she* was the victim."

"We thought so too, sir, but actually...*you* were the intended victim all along," responded one of the officers.

William and I looked at each other, the both of us perplexed to say the least.

"I don't get it," William said.

"Well, Mr. Figlit, the first piece to the puzzle came to us just three days ago when we found Mr. Pantaloni's car parked in the woods off the main county road, damn near Leather Junction."

As William and I sat down, my brother invited the officers to do the same.

"Please, gentlemen, take a seat," he said. "I don't believe I'll be able to remain on my feet for this."

"Are you all right, Mr. Figlit?" asked one of the officers. "Do you need a glass of water?"

"No, no, I'm fine," said my brother with a wave of his hand, ready to listen.

William's apprehension was clearly evident as he braced himself for what promised to be a bizarre account. It called for his undivided attention in the strictest, most thorough sense of the expression. Given this, he sat on the edge of his seat and listened carefully in an attempt to fully grasp the utter...*absurdity* of it all.

***

Debbie and Christine had a plan of which the main goal was to ruin William but, of course, each girl had her own reason. Naturally, Debbie was the more bitter of the two, given the fact that William had unceremoniously severed their relationship, toxic though it was. She also felt that she had invested what she considered to be precious time and heartfelt emotion. Her argument against what William had done to her remained consistent and in that she would *never* change her tune, expressing the same litany of complaints over and over again. Hadn't she been patient when his mother got sick? Wasn't she understanding when William had to sleep on his mother's couch to keep her from walking off into the night or falling headlong into the creek, ranting and raving like a lunatic? He promised they would get married when the time was right...when his mother was no longer an issue. Well, now the crazy old woman was gone and William went back on his promise. How dare he do that to her? His duplicity was not only unacceptable, but humiliating as well. Debbie would not be disgraced like that in front of her family and friends. As a matter of fact, she was sure that the whole damn county would soon be gossiping that yet another boyfriend had dumped Deborah Mead. And so, as always, she ranted and raved...on and on and on.

Christine, on the other hand, had a different reason for wanting to punish William. After all, she *never* had a problem attracting boys...or men. If she was not the center of attention, she made damn sure that she maneuvered herself into some sort of spotlight where the opposite sex might be inclined to flock in greater numbers. Of course, they would soon discover that Christine had several undesirable character traits that would drive them away expeditiously.

First of all, she flirted with unabashed determination with whoever would take the bait. There were times when she had two or three fellows on tender hooks at the same time. What guy wanted to play second fiddle to another guy? Secondly, she was as shallow as the day was long...not a sincere bone in her body. This dashed anyone's hope of ever entering into an earnest relationship with Christine. She would never know how to go about it! Most notably, she was a spoiler who enjoyed coming between any two people who appeared to have a strong relationship. This she did for the mere sake of it...or the challenge of it...or the fun of it. Finally, she was an all-around, no-doubt-about-it, lowly, dirty cheat...plain and simple. Christine's mother had sent her to her Aunt Debbie for all of these reasons and more, for there was no controlling the girl who attempted to use her wiles on William too...but he would not take the bait.

So each woman, scorned and rejected by the same man, would play a part in exacting sweet revenge. It would be an elaborate yet most compendious hoax, carried out with precision for the express purpose of ruining William for the rest of his life...or close to it. They felt that it was the perfect plan, impenetrable as a matter of fact, and sure to achieve the desired result. It was for this that each woman acted out her role with high expectations and relish, knowing full well that when it was all over, they will have destroyed a man simply because he distanced himself from each of them, albeit for different reasons. For the life of them, the possibility of failing to successfully carry out their ruse had never entered their minds, a sure sign of their deviance...and stupidity.

Debbie and Christine launched their wicked plan in William's apartment only minutes after he had gone to be with Tilly and Skeet. When they were sure that Mr. Pantaloni was away from his store window, otherwise and sufficiently occupied with sewing, mending and the like, Debbie and Christine crept up the back stairs and gained entry with the key that Debbie vowed never to relinquish. They knew they would have to be quick about their business, for Mr. Pantaloni was a fast worker who loved to nose around the property after putting down his needle and thread, but they wanted him to hear...hear *everything*.

After the two women were within the confines of the kitchen, Debbie secured the lock on the back door once more. Immediately and with particular relish, they began to barrage each other with epithets most foul, calling each other horrible names and so forth. Of course, Mr. Pantaloni *knew* the sound of Debbie's voice and the two hoped that if Christine's caustic words were expressed in a guttural, deep-throated fashion then maybe, just maybe, he would think that he was listening to yet another argument between William and Debbie. After all, those disputes were becoming a near daily occurrence. What else would he possibly think?

After the initial outpouring of vitriol, Christine kept her contribution of nasty words to a minimum, giving Debbie the predominance in the scathing war of words. This was something that she usually had over William anyway. Could they fool Mr. Pantaloni? Could they make him naturally assume that the offensive exchange...the growling, howling, and snarling...was actually taking place between William and Debbie? The tailor had certainly heard his share of disputes in the past between the two and would say as much, for he would always make some kind of comment to William the following day. He would never mention anything to Debbie, though. He was afraid of *her*.

"Mama mia, William!" Mr. Pantaloni would say. "That

was some fight the two of you had last night! I'm surprised you are still able to stand!"

What Debbie and Christine were also counting on, of course, was that Mr. Pantaloni would stay downstairs, this being his usual practice. Maybe it was just apprehension or, perhaps, his fear of Debbie that kept the nervous little tailor from ever coming upstairs to investigate a loud fight, for he never interfered in the frequent showdowns between William and Debbie. Also, Debbie felt that she knew Mr. Pantaloni pretty well and was confident that if, in fact, he had seen William leave the apartment to be with Tilly and Skeet, then he would just assume that William had returned for some reason or another and could not avoid a fight. At any rate, the naïve tailor would never attempt to analyze it; as a matter of fact, he probably wouldn't give it a second thought.

So, the two women continued to perpetrate a ruse that they were convinced could work, its sole purpose to destroy William...and they reveled in doing so.

As they swore, accused, and damned each other to hell, they simultaneously broke whatever they could get their hands on: dishes, bric-a-brac, two lamps, a flower vase, a small footstool, and a kitchen chair. Within mere seconds, there was extensive breakage and the apartment itself had sustained damage to the floors and walls. Then, without even flinching, Debbie took one of William's pocketknives out of her small purse and promptly sliced the index finger of her left hand...right down the middle. She let out a small scream, but smiled at the immediate flow of rich, red blood that dripped from her finger as she walked from room to room after having placed the bloody knife back into her purse.

After writing William's initials in blood on the bathroom mirror, Debbie turned the gas back on at the main valve, flooding the apartment with the noxious fuel by way of the four stovetop burners. Both Debbie and Christine then hurriedly exited the apartment through the kitchen door and down the back staircase, grabbing William's work shirt that hung on the hook behind the door as they left. The two women were positively giddy about what they had just done, proof that their intentional reckless behavior gave them a great sense of self-satisfaction with William's ultimate ruin never far from their minds.

Debbie continued to drip blood as she descended the stairs and walked out of the back door before wrapping her bleeding finger in William's work shirt. She quickly got into her car and took the bloody pocketknife back out of her purse, placing it in the visor above the steering wheel in such a way that it would easily be spotted. Her finger still wrapped, Debbie then sped off.

In the meantime, Christine ran over to Mr. Pantaloni's car, always parked out of site of the tailor shop behind a large tree near the back corner of the property, and jumped into the driver's seat. Now, Mr. Pantaloni had once let it be known, in a quiet sort of way, that he always kept the key in the ignition just in case he had to get away quickly from Mrs. Pantaloni. Debbie did not believe *that* for one minute, figuring that his leaving the key was one of Mr. Pantaloni's bad habits or, perhaps, wishful thinking on his part that the car would actually be stolen one day for it was an old, rusted out bomb. Debbie knew, however, that the big heap would fit perfectly into their plan.

Having already made certain that the key was in the ignition, just as Mr. Pantaloni had stated, Christine carried out the criminal task of stealing the old rattletrap and following Debbie out to the main county road. There, Debbie removed William's bloodstained shirt from around her sliced finger and stuffed it under the driver's seat. After wrapping her finger tightly in a bandage taken from her purse, she quickly hopped out from behind the wheel and climbed into Mr. Pantaloni's car with Christine at the helm. The two women then fled toward Leather Junction without looking back, thinking they had ingeniously pulled off their ruse.

Once they reached the end of the main county road, Christine purposely drove into the woods and parked in an isolated spot behind a large boulder whereby she and Debbie covered the old vehicle with brush taken from the broken branches of a felled tree. The police were tipped-off about this shoddy attempt at camouflage by two boys who happened to be hunting in that neck of the woods the very next day while, at the same time, the women's plan to ruin William had all but failed when they were picked up by a squad car as they aimlessly walked the Leather Junction causeway. Their story of a harrowing escape from William's clutches was inconsistent at best and unraveled quickly... practically before they even got out of the car at the police station.

***

William and I looked at each other in utter disbelief.

"That is the most ridiculous story I have ever heard in my entire life," William commented in shock.

"Their plan was obviously flawed in more ways than one,

and they were completely naïve to think that they could actually get away with it," said one of the officers, shaking his head.

"And how exactly did they intend to ruin me with this ridiculous charade?" asked William incredulously.

"They tried to make it look as though you had killed Miss Mead or, at the very least, had harmed her in some violent way," answered the other officer.

"Then what were they going to do...where were they going to go?" asked William angrily. "What was the next step in their plan? Did they think they could just walk off into the sunset on the Leather Junction causeway?"

William's questions came fast and furiously. He was absolutely incensed and I did not blame him one bit.

"I don't think that they had gotten that far in their thinking," the first officer conjectured. "When we picked them up they were obviously attempting to flee the area. What they planned on doing after that, we just don't know. Neither woman can come up with a straight answer. That alone tells us that they had no plans beyond the Leather Junction causeway."

William and I were both flabbergasted.

"Now what?" asked William as he stood up from his chair. "Well, these women have numerous charges filed against them, some of them quite serious," commented one officer. "We're looking at grand theft auto, criminal mischief, conspiracy to commit a crime, reckless endangerment, and contributing to the delinquency of a minor...just to name a few. They'll both be going away...that's for sure."

"And they both willingly admitted to what they did?" William asked curiously.

"Actually, sir, they tripped and stumbled over their story right from the start, so much so that it was no trouble getting confessions out of either of them," the other officer said. "So it appears, Mr. Figlit, that you are free and clear to move about as you please as you are no longer suspect of any wrong doing. We have all we need from the apartment, so you're free to go back there too. The only thing is, you have a massive cleanup ahead of you when you get there."

At that point, both William and I were too shocked to say or ask anything further.

"Thank you for your time, sir," the officer said graciously as the two men stood up. "Goodbye ma'am," he said as he tipped his hat in my direction.

William walked the two officers to the door and with that, they left my apartment.

"We'll be in touch if we need you or have anything further to report," one officer said over his shoulder as both men walked down the hallway and got onto the elevator.

William closed the door to the apartment and looked at me with wide eyes.

"I still can't believe *any* of this," he said, wiping the sweat off of his forehead with a handkerchief. "It's like something out of a movie."

"You beat the wrap, Baby Face," I said kiddingly to my brother. "Now, you can go home and carry on with your life. Those two crazy women won't ever bother you again."

"Do you *really* think that Mr. Pantaloni will allow me to return to that apartment?" William asked, already sure of the answer.

"If he doesn't, you can come live in the city with Skeet and me after we sell Ma's house and split the proceeds ...

where we can be together...as a family," I said, placing my hand on William's arm. "And I can be certain that you'll meet a lovely girl and get married," I added for further enticement.

"I think I've had it with women for a while," William said dryly.

I smiled and patted him on the back.

"C'mon, let's go back to the hospital to see Skeet," I said, still smiling.

As we were about to leave the apartment, there came another knock at the door.

"What now?" William said impatiently.

He opened the door to find my next door neighbor, Victoria Coogan, standing there with a piece of my mail that had been accidentally placed in her mailbox...and a batch of brownies.

"I'm sorry to bother the two of you," Victoria began, "but your mail got mixed in again with mine, Tilly, and I thought that you might appreciate...well, here...I baked some brownies. Please enjoy them."

Victoria handed a small white envelope to me, and a plateful of brownies to William. The two exchanged sweet smiles as their eyes locked.

"Thank you...for these," William said, shyly stumbling over his words.

"You're quite welcome," said Victoria quietly.

Their gazes were still fixed on one another. I detected sparks.

"Well, as I said...enjoy them," said Victoria, snapping out of her trance as she awkwardly turned to leave.

"Yes, I will...I mean *we* will," William answered brightly. "Please, stop by again," he said with a smile, slowly closing the door as he watched Victoria walk down the hallway.

She looked over her shoulder and smiled at William one more time before he shut the door completely. To say that my brother was captivated would be an understatement.

"Smitten are we?" I said, teasing him.

"I have *got* to go home as soon as possible," William said, ignoring my question.

He was shaking his head, but had a broad smile on his face as he stuffed a brownie into his mouth.

"What is your hurry?" I asked. "The mess that awaits you is not going anywhere."

"Forget the mess," he said through a mouthful of chocolate fudge brownie. "I need to sell Ma's house...quickly."

William continued to smile as he stuffed another brownie into his mouth. Life had suddenly taken a turn...a very sweet turn.

Chapter 22

It's Me...Tilly

I wonder by my troth, what thou and I did, till we loved?
Were we not weaned till then?

—John Donne, *The Good Morrow*

The days went by much more easily now as Skeet's health continued to improve. He no longer appeared pale and got up every morning on his own, dressing in what he liked to call his *going home clothes*. He enjoyed his food again and reveled in the occasional burger and fries from the hospital cafeteria. He gently shaved his boyish face every day now, and combed his thick brown hair, which had grown back with a bit of a curl. He was obviously feeling well and more like himself, so it was no big surprise, but entirely welcome, when Flanders Trumbull told us the good news.

"Skeet's latest blood draw indicates that his bone marrow is making blood cells and platelets in sufficient numbers. I am very pleased."

Thank goodness. It finally appeared that we were coming to the end of the long, long road. Dunnith Nelligan's death had certainly scared Skeet, and may have even dealt him an emotional setback for a few days, but in the end it had taught him to stay strong and always look to the future with hope and determination. That is what Dunnith Nelligan did, even though he probably knew in the back of his young mind that he would not live to see another year. Skeet would never forget him.

When Flanders told Skeet that he could finally go home we all cried tears of joy, including William who, in the midst of personal turmoil and domestic conflict, had saved his brother's life. Of course, Skeet would still have to be seen in the outpatient clinic just about every day for several weeks so that all aspects of his blood and overall health could be properly monitored. He could not yet frequent public places and Flanders told him that he must still wear a mask, most definitely when he visited the clinic and probably before going anywhere else. This annoyed Skeet because he hated wearing the mask, but Flanders made no bones about it.

"If you catch a virus or pick up an infection, you may incur dangerous complications as a result," Flanders said pointedly. "Remember that your immune system is still recovering. Use common sense for a while, pamper yourself...and *do not* overdo things."

Flanders Trumbull was adamant. Skeet had come too far to get reckless with his health now.

"Also, I assume that you will be getting a few visitors," the doctor continued.

"I suppose so," Skeet shrugged, not having thought about it.

"Well, I know that you are not going to like this, but you will also have to wear it at home too," Flanders instructed.

"At home?" Skeet whined. "Are you kidding me?"

"Not only when you have company, but until your apartment has been sanitized according to my instructions," the doctor added for good measure.

Skeet was bitterly disappointed, but Flanders Trumbull

wouldn't yield on the issue.

"How long will I have to wear the stupid thing, especially at home?" Skeet asked, still whining like a small child.

"Until I tell you otherwise, my friend, but you should only have to wear it for a short while," insisted Flanders, slightly smiling at Skeet's childish reaction.

"What does that mean?" asked Skeet.

"It means that you will probably have to wear it until you have finished your round of examinations and tests at the outpatient clinic," Flanders said. "If everything stays positive, as I suspect it will, you will then be free to discontinue wearing it."

"I'll see to it that he follows your instructions to the letter, Flan," I said.

Flanders gave me a quick, appreciative wink and left the room. I knew that Skeet would probably have to be poked and prodded on a regular basis for the rest of his life, a relatively small price to pay, I suppose, for cheating death. But it was obvious that after so long an ordeal had nearly come to an end, he did not want to be immersed in the pitfalls of sickness, mortality, and hair loss any longer. He was ready to move forward.

Over the next several weeks, Skeet went to the outpatient clinic faithfully. His blood counts were always perfect and he was staying healthy. Flanders Trumbull was, once again, quite pleased with himself but he had complimentary words for Skeet too.

"You are a good patient, Skeet," said Flanders. "You have followed all of my instructions and suggestions faithfully. Pretty soon, you won't need to see me anymore and then... you will miss me terribly."

142

"Like a crutch," Skeet replied with a wry smile.

But he knew. Flanders Trumbull had saved his life.

Soon the day came when Skeet, with Flan's permission, asked me to take a road trip...a special road trip.

"You, William, and I will be going," he told me. "William will do the driving. Trust me...you'll love it."

Beyond that, both men acted quite mysteriously, refusing to give me any further information except...

"You might want to fancy up a little...maybe even wear a pretty dress," Skeet told me, anticipating my resistance.

"A dress? Really? You know I don't like to wear dresses," I scoffed. "C'mon...what is this? Tell me what's going on here."

"Trust me Fig," said Skeet. "Just trust me."

He was almost giddy.

The day came and Skeet felt better than he had in a long, long time. He wore a nice pair of pants and a white button-down dress shirt while I wore the only dress I owned...a casual, blue cotton chemise with tiny white flowers. Skeet said I looked beautiful.

"Let us be off," said William, a dapper looking chauffer who delighted in keeping Skeet's secret from me. He teased me mercilessly as we drove, my curiosity becoming almost unmanageable.

"Just enjoy the drive, sweetheart," Skeet said as he placed his arm around my shoulders and gave me a sweet peck on the cheek.

We looked like a couple of turtledoves sitting in that back seat as my heart raced with anticipation.

We drove into the County, that all too familiar terrain that the three of us knew so well. It was the place upon which all of our childhood memories were founded, both precious and abhorrent, and no matter where life took any one of us it would always be called *home*. Expectedly, the drive was long and hot, but picturesque. Miles and miles of farmland streamed effortlessly into the cloudless blue horizon while the valleys heaved their billowy morning mist. We drove the familiar Jepson Highway over Leet Hill onto Chapel Road. There stood the little white church as it always had, off to the right and high upon the hill, its stained glass windows gleaming in the sun.

"We're going home?" I asked curiously.

Skeet smiled and squeezed my hand.

Once we were at the end of Chapel Road, we turned onto the nameless dirt drive that led to Ma's house. The tiny ranch in which William and I grew up appeared before us, the For Sale sign situated on the small patch of grass out front flapping in the gentle breeze.

"Why are we at Ma's house?" I inquired before any of us exited the car.

William just smiled at me as he looked over his shoulder into the back seat, never saying a word. Skeet gently took me by the hand.

"C'mon, Fig," he said smiling. "I want to show you something."

We got out of the car and walked into the backyard; I never even realized that William had stayed behind.

"What is it that you want to show me?" I asked. "Everything back here looks just the same as it did the last time we were here."

"I guess I just want to relive things a bit," Skeet said sentimentally.

Ever since he had gotten out of the hospital, I tried to accommodate every little desire or request, given what he had just been through. He appeared to be more joyous now than I think I had ever seen him before, this road trip doing him a world of good.

"We *did* spend some fun times back here, didn't we?" I admitted, happily recalling some of our shenanigans.

"It was the best part of my childhood," Skeet acknowledged.

Ma's spirit from the good old days, when she was a strong and resolute Christian woman raising a little girl alone, seemed to follow us about the yard. We walked down to the creek and watched the swift current of clear water as it babbled over the rocks and stones. For only a fleeting moment did I flash back to the disturbing memory of lighting Sheffield LeMay's old, bloody red bandana afire on the bank of the creek and scattering its ashes with my bare hands over the running waters. This I did to protect Ma...without reservation. It was my memory and mine alone, dispelled quickly by all of Skeet's beautiful remembrances of our growing up... and falling in love. There were now many precious and wonderful reasons why the dark aspects of my life should no longer have a place in my head.

"Remember how we used to share licks on those all-day cherry suckers?" Skeet reminded me with a broad smile. "And how I taught you to skip stones across the creek waters? Remember that, Fig?" he gently chuckled.

"I do," I said laughing, "and I also remember playing those silly harmonicas."

"*Southern Hoe Down Medley* and *Sweet Night Lullaby*, our two favorite songs!" he recalled with glee.

"The only two songs we *knew* how to play!" I happily emphasized.

A warm and tender feeling came over me as Skeet took both of my hands and pulled me close. It had been such a long time since we were romantic, since we had flirted with one another, since he had said...

"I love you, Fig. Let's get married."

"I love you too and I already said I'd marry you," I giggled.

"No, I mean right here, right now," said Skeet, pulling a marriage license out of his pocket.

My eyes widened. I was delightedly surprised.

"I had to wheedle the county clerk," Skeet said, referring to the document in his hand. "C'mon, honey," he said softly. "Let's tie the knot just as we had planned."

"You mean right here in the backyard?" I smiled.

"Right here by the creek," Skeet confirmed as he watched William and the newest reverend from the little white church come walking into the backyard.

William carried a beautiful bouquet of white roses, handing them over to me after kissing my cheek. He then stepped back, proudly watching as my future unfolded.

"This is where it all began, honey...where we shared so much together...where we fell in love," Skeet said softly with hopeful anticipation.

He was gentle and tender, but his eyes burned with a driven passion. I melted into his arms and readily agreed.

The reverend married us on the spot where we exchanged sweet words and lifelong promises as Skeet slipped a simple band of gold over my engagement ring. It was all too brief, yet it sealed our shared destiny for all eternity. And for a fleeting moment, a gentle breeze blew Ma's loving whisper

146

into my ear.

"Congratulations!" exclaimed William as he hugged me tightly and gave Skeet a hearty handshake. "Much good health and happiness to the both of you for a long, long time."

We all lingered by the creek for a few minutes longer before sauntering back to William's parked car. The reverend insisted upon walking back to the little white church, the day being so clear and pleasant. Skeet and I climbed into the backseat of the car like two giddy teenagers, getting downright silly when he pulled an all-day cherry sucker from his shirt pocket. We shared licks as though we were kids all over again while Skeet excitedly talked about our future together...a future he never thought he would get the chance to see. I listened with enchantment to his every word and I was charmed as I had never been before...and very much in love. I brought the beautiful bouquet of white roses to my face and gently breathed in its sweet fragrance. It was all so lovely, so breathtaking...so magical.

"...And we'll have a house, and a couple of kids, and maybe even a dog," Skeet rambled, stopping briefly to take a breath.

William turned around from the driver's seat and interrupted before Skeet could continue his litany of future hopes and dreams.

"Where to next?" he asked.

"How are you feeling, sweetheart?" I asked Skeet. "Are you tired?"

"I could climb a mountain," he replied. "What do you have in mind?"

I gingerly made my request, so afraid that it might spoil

the day.

"I'd like to stop by the cemetery to pay a visit to Ma ...if you don't mind. It will only take me a few minutes," I promised.

"I don't mind at all," Skeet assured me, lifting my hand to his lips and kissing it softly. "I understand and when we get there...you take your time."

At that point, I think he would have given me the moon if he could.

Skeet instructed William to drive to our mother's resting place.

"To the cemetery it is," said William, nodding his head in compliance.

I would be forever grateful to my brother for so many reasons and on so many different levels. I may not have known him well during his growing up years, but I want to know him now. He is my family, Skeet's lifesaver, and a tangible link to Ma. I want to keep him close and give him everything I can...as a sister and a friend. He deserves every happiness because that is what he has made possible for Skeet and me.

As we pulled up to the cemetery, I took in a deep breath. It had, indeed, been a long and arduous road since we first learned of Skeet's illness. Those long days that had stretched into weeks of not knowing whether or not he would actually pull through his illness elicited in me a longing for my mother. If there was ever a time in my life when I needed her comfort and support it was then. And, of course, I would have given anything to have her *physically* by my side today. I needed to talk to her, remember her as she had been...before the darkness, before the demons had snatched her away.

"Do you want me to walk over to the grave with you?"

Skeet asked.

"No," I answered, smiling at him as I cupped his cheek in my hand. "I'd appreciate it if the two of you would just wait in the car. I'll only be a couple of minutes."

"Take your time, Tilly," said William. "There is no hurry."

"I'll be right here if you need me, sweetheart," Skeet assured me.

The two of them could not have been more understanding.

My feeling of blissful exhilaration having temporarily subsided, I walked over to Ma's grave and stood in front of her headstone:

Thanks for being there with me today, Ma. Were you pleased? Were you proud? There is not a day goes by that I don't think of you...feel your motherly touch...hear your loving advice...because you are always with me...in my heart. I wanted you to know that. I love you, Ma. It's me...Tilly.

A single tear trickled slowly down my cheek as I laid my wedding bouquet of white roses in front of Ma's headstone and gently touched its hard surface, tracing the letters of her name with my fingers. I smiled and contentedly turned away, having said all I needed to say.

As I walked back toward the car, I could see Skeet watching me...and smiling. My feeling of blissful exhilaration having returned, I quickened my step. He got out of the car as I approached and wrapped me in his arms.

"Are you okay?" Skeet asked, wiping the wetness from my cheek with his hand.

"I'm just fine, darling," I answered, kissing him softly. "Just fine."

We both climbed into the backseat of the car, ready to

149

embark upon our wonderful future together as husband and wife. As William slowly drove out of the cemetery I never looked back, and at no time would I visit Ma's resting place... ever again.

Chapter 23

What a Time It Was

Clocks slay time...only when the clock stops does time come to life.

— William Faulkner, *The Sound and the Fury*

We stopped briefly at the tailor shop before heading back to the city. William wanted desperately to speak with Mr. Pantaloni and survey the damage to his apartment. He felt awful about what had happened and longed to convey his feelings to the kindly tailor who had been victimized by the ordeal as well. My brother also intended to tell him that he was finally ready to leave the County behind and make a fresh start.

"Mr. Pantaloni, I must apologize for everything that has happened. I feel completely responsible," William said with sincere remorse, even though he had done nothing wrong.

I suppose that, in a way, he was apologizing for being involved with a woman like Debbie...for even bringing her to live in his apartment. After all, prior to her moving in, life for William had been pretty peaceful until Ma got sick, and the good-natured Mr. Pantaloni appreciated having a reserved bachelor living upstairs, especially one who paid his monthly rent on time. Now, the apartment that William had come to love was sadly unlivable. His shock upon seeing the havoc that Debbie and Christine had wreaked within the walls of his home brought tears to his eyes. He felt an emotional mix of anger and sadness, but his concern *really* centered on Mr. Pantaloni.

William felt badly upon observing the old tailor's obvious stress and emotional upset over the entire upstairs incident, not to mention the fact that his car had been stolen too.

"I'll clean the mess and repair the damage myself," William assured him. "It will look as good as new in no time."

"Thank you, William," Mr. Pantaloni said, looking as grave as grave could be. "Those two women must never come back here again," he said, visibly shaken by his own mention of them.

"They will *never* come back here again, I can promise you that," William said.

My brother had a genuine affection for Mr. Pantaloni, the kind one would have for a good-natured uncle. That is why he felt awful over what he was about to say next.

"Mr. Pantaloni, I've decided to move away to the city where I'll be closer to my family," William began. "I think that will be best for everyone and you'll have no problem finding another tenant. I need to move on with my life," William explained quietly with a friendly hand on Mr. Pantaloni's shoulder.

"What will you do in the city?" asked the concerned tailor. "Mama mia, it is so big and noisy there!"

Mr. Pantaloni put a hand to his head.

"I'll find work, perhaps at the hospital where my sister is a doctor," William said hopefully.

The two men looked at each other with sad eyes.

"You have lived here a long time," said Mr. Pantaloni, "and you have always been a good tenant. I wish you *buona fortuna*."

The two men touchingly embraced, much like a father and son, before William walked back to the car where Skeet and I were waiting, still sharing licks on our dwindling all-day cherry sucker. Before getting into the car, William looked back over his shoulder at Mr. Pantaloni.

"I'll return in three days," he called out. "Don't worry about the apartment...please. I'll take care of everything."

The two then waved goodbye as William got into the car and drove off. It had been an eventful day that encompassed every emotion known to the human spirit and, hopefully, propelled our little family into a promising future with no further secrets...and no more heartache.

The three of us talked all the way home. William excitedly informed me that today, before the wedding ceremony took place, the newest reverend from the little white church had made a substantial offer on Ma's house. This welcome bit of news clearly explained why my brother no longer wavered between remaining in the County and moving to the city, a decision he was secretly grappling with even though he knew it was the right thing to do. The considerable offer had ultimately pushed him into making that life-changing decision, one that he would never regret. We readily agreed with one another that selling Ma's house to the reverend would be the best course of action for everyone concerned. It looked as though finally, life had taken a turn for the better...in our direction!

When we got home after our long drive, William packed a bag.

"I'll be back as soon as I can," he told me.

"The County no longer holds its charms for you, does it?"

I asked him rhetorically.

"You know, I'm actually anxious...no, make that excited...to leave that piece of my life behind," William reflected. "It's a chapter I'll never seek to deny, but refuse to wallow in by remaining in the County any longer. Let's face it, Debbie's scolding words would forever taunt me in that apartment; thoughts of the Reverend Chauncey repeatedly pounding my head against the cold stone floor of the little white church when I was a kid would inevitably invade my mind every time I worshipped there; and Ma...well...her haunted ramblings in that tiny white house in which we both grew up would continue to play over and over again in my head, spooking me all over again, unless we get rid of the place...once and for all."

I was moved by my brother's retrospection, a rather tragic tale of abuse and heartache, courageously and poignantly recounted.

William would see my neighbor, Victoria Coogan, before he left.

"I have some loose ends to tie up back home in the County," he informed her, "but then I'll be returning here for good. I was wondering if you and I could have dinner together when I get back."

William felt butterflies in his stomach that he had not felt in a long, long time.

"I would love to have dinner with you," Victoria said softly.

The sparks that flew between them were obvious and strong. My brother gave her a bright smile and a spontaneous peck on the cheek. She smiled too, and blushed a little, as he offered a quick *goodbye* and walked away.

Before William left for the County, however, Skeet spoke to him once again of his undying gratitude.

"You've already thanked me," William said with a smile and a gentle pat on Skeet's arm. "You're my brother. You don't have to thank me any further."

"I could never thank you *enough*," Skeet contradicted him, "and I want you to know that you are welcome to live with Tilly and me until you find a place of your own. You will always have a place here. Always."

"Thanks, brother," William said gratefully. "That's good to know."

"And it might not be such a bad thing, you know... being Victoria's neighbor," Skeet said teasingly.

"Not a bad thing at all," William reflected with an amused, far away gleam in his eye. "Not a bad thing at all."

William kept his word to Mr. Pantaloni and returned to the County three days later to clean up and repair his bloodied, damaged apartment above the tailor shop. He also gave the place a fresh coat of paint for good measure, making it look as good as new. It would take him a couple of weeks, but it had turned out so well that Mr. Pantaloni was able to rent it almost immediately to one of his steady customers, a Mr. Giorgio Camicia, who had just recently lost his wife. In a way, William was sorry to leave the flat, now brighter and cleaner than ever before, but Mr. Pantaloni was clearly pleased about his new tenant.

"It will be nice to have a paisan upstairs," he commented.

William arranged for the three of us to travel back to the County just one more time for both Ma's memorial service at the little white church and the closing on her house. The reverend graciously agreed to conduct the service in the morning and sign off on the house in the afternoon, thereby officially taking it off our hands and making it his own. This allowed us to leave the County with no loose ends, effectively cutting all of our ties forever. There would never again be a reason to return...ever. As for Ma, her body may have been buried in a remote section of the County Cemetery, but her indomitable human spirit would return to the city...with all of us.

***

Oh, those long ago days are forever etched in my memory and pictured so vividly, so boldly. The secrets...the intrigue... the suspicion captivate me still, not to mention the mystery and grief. And the worry...I will never forget the worry! You were there, darling...we lived through it all...together...you and I.

"That's right, my Fig," Skeet says again while still stroking my hair. "Keep your eyes closed. Relax. Relax. Think of nothing else but getting better...and you will."

I was back there again, darling...what a time it was in both of our lives...what a time it was...in both...of...our...lives.

"Nurse! Nurse!" Skeet cries out. "Come quickly!"

"What is it, Mr. LeMay?" asks the nurse in an alarmed voice as she comes rushing into my room.

My eyes are wide open and I can see Skeet standing over me.

"It's my wife," he says with tears in his eyes and a stunned expression. "She's...she's...smiling."

Chapter 24

A Family...Tight and True

So now faith, hope, and love abide, these three;
but the greatest of these is love.

—The *Bible*, 1 Corinthians 13:13

And so it goes. First, I can move one finger...then two... then three. In a week's time I can pick up a glass with either hand, sit up in bed, and wiggle the toes on both feet. The nurses and physical therapists have me moving, reaching, grasping and stretching daily. Skeet is a wonderful cheerleader, always by my side or holding my hand as I learn how to put one foot in front of the other all over again. In the meantime, someone else holds me steady by the waistband of my pants as I walk with a walker up and down the hallway...up and down...up and down. My right foot still turns a little when I walk and feels a bit more numbed than I care to admit. It isn't always easy to bend my right knee either. Oh, I *tell* it to bend, but it doesn't always listen. So, I walk up and down the hallway...up and down...up and down... forcing my knee to listen, my foot to point straight.

My hands are strong, though, and listen quite well when I will them to do something. I can pick up this or grasp that. I can catch, throw, point, and squeeze. My hands are good listeners...very cooperative. They give me hope for a complete recovery.

"I love you," says Skeet as he holds my hand and squeezes it, and I squeeze back...because I can.

"I l-love y-you t-too," I stammer.

Sometimes, I close my eyes tight when I have trouble getting a word out. I then force my brain and scrunch my face. Skeet says it's like getting the last bit of toothpaste out of the tube...only harder. To me, it's more like squeezing a sliver out of a finger...only harder.

"That's right," says Skeet smiling. "Keep driving those words right out of your head and through your mouth... push, push, push."

That is easy for him to say. Not that I don't appreciate the encouragement but sometimes, no matter how hard I force my brain and scrunch my face, I just can't get the toothpaste out of the tube...or the sliver out of the finger.

So, I begin working with a speech therapist: ba, ba, ba... ma, ma, ma...pa, pa, pa...ta, ta, ta. This I do every single day for a fixed period of time and more often than not, twice a day when the therapist feels that I can handle it. I find it silly and embarrassing, but I am told that I must be diligent in order to regain my speech. Deep down inside I know this is true, so during those rare times when I have complete privacy in my room, I practice those funny sounds all by myself. All in all it is a tedious regimen, this learning how to walk and talk again, and I get increasingly impatient because I want everything back...everything that I lost...*right now*. Taking the initiative to practice those funny sounds and walk up and down the hallway...up and down...up and down... gives me a sense of control over my own destiny, for my perseverance will only serve to get me out of here sooner. This I know.

And so the days go.

"She is doing much better," Skeet says to the nurse, nodding his head.

"Much better," the nurse concurs with a smile. "Look at her go."

Thankfully, after days of forcing and scrunching, squeezing and pushing, walking up and down the hallway with a walker...up and down...up and down...and endless utterances of ba, ma, pa, ta, I can now speak with much less frustration and walk steadily with a cane. To me, my progress is miraculous, and it has everyone quite pleased and surprised at the relatively short amount of time that it took me to regain my movement and speech. Hopefully, this marked improvement is my ticket out of this place.

"I want to g-go home," I inform Skeet. "I am ready."

"Soon, sweetheart, very soon," he says.

It cannot be soon enough. There are a few more days of therapy, walking, talking and paperwork, but all of the hard work finally pays off when they tell me I can leave. The thought of going home to be with Skeet again gives me boundless joy.

"You have done quite well for yourself, Doctor Figlit," the nurse tells me. "You're a real fighter. Congratulations."

"Aging can be d-difficult sometimes," I say, waxing philosophical.

The young nurse sympathizes, but doesn't really know... not now...not yet.

"Our ride is here," announces Skeet, gently taking my hand in his. "It's time to go."

I have been waiting for those words for, what seems, an eternity.

"Thank g-goodness," I declare. "I hope I r-recognize the place."

"Oh, you will," Skeet reassures me.

He holds a beautiful bouquet of colorful wildflowers in his other hand, a lovely thought from a man who has been completely preoccupied with a sick wife.

"You know who these are for, don't you," Skeet comments, flashing his signature smile...the smile I fell in love with all those years ago.

"I sure d-do," I immediately confirm while sitting myself down in the required wheelchair that will transport me to the front door of the hospital. "I am r-ready. Let's go," I instruct the nurse who will do all the pushing.

Skeet keeps in step with the rolling chair, glancing down at me every so often. He whistles a nondescript tune, a sure sign that he is relaxed and contented, while carefully clutching his wildflowers.

As we roll along, I can see William and Victoria anxiously awaiting us in the lobby, my brother pacing and jiggling the change in his pocket. They are a Godsend to Skeet and me, the best brother and sister-in-law anyone could ever hope to have. They watch out for us and we cherish them. We are a family...tight and true. Our years together have been nothing short of a blessing.

"With more to come," Skeet assures me.

And why not? We have beaten the odds time and time again our entire lives...Skeet, William, and I. It is my belief that angels sit permanently upon our shoulders.

"Hello, you two," William says brightly as he approaches my wheelchair.

He takes my hand and affectionately kisses me on the

cheek. Skeet and Victoria lock arms, pleased that brother and sister are united once more for a most happy occasion... my homecoming.

The nurse wheels me to the front door of the hospital and stops, allowing Skeet and William to help me out of the chair. With a smile and a wave, I say my goodbyes.

"Th-thank you for everything, d-dear," I say. "You have b-been wonderful."

On the arms of my husband and brother, I take the few short steps to William's car that awaits us in the circular drive of the hospital.

"Where to?" William asks. "Shall we go dancing?"

"Not before we make our yearly stop," Skeet reminds him.

"Oh, yes of course," says William obligingly.

"Th-Thank you, William," I say appreciatively. "You know h-how important it is to us."

"I do," my brother verifies with a solemn nod. "I most certainly do."

***

William drives us away from the hospital, his reflexes taut...his eyes watchful and alert. The city is active this fine day as hundreds of people move along the sidewalks in one fluid motion while the congested streets are particularly challenging, even for a sharp driver like William. He faces the traffic obstacles with steadfast precision, though, masterfully navigating the road as he taxis us toward the city outskirts. Thankfully, he drives us most places now. Skeet still drives but only occasionally, while I don't know if I'll ever have the dexterity to drive again. William insists that we rely on him to get around, saying that he doesn't mind taking us wherever we need to go. He has never come right out and said it, but I know he thinks that Skeet and I are both too old to be behind the wheel anymore. Maybe he's right.

We quickly reach the city's periphery where William turns onto the long, winding road that stretches for mile after pretty mile. Eventually, the grassy knolls and gentle slopes give way to a vast cemetery with its neatly fenced in head-stones and meticulously manicured lawns and shrubbery. We drive into the expansive resting place and turn down a short, evenly paved side road that leads us to our destination.

Skeet and I get out of the car, just the two of us, and slowly walk over to a grave that is conveniently close to the road. Still clutching the colorful bouquet of wildflowers, Skeet bends down and carefully places them in front of the white marble headstone that aptly reads:

Doctor Flanders Trumbull

Heroic and Noble Healer
Guardian and Defender of the Sick
Friend to All

We smile at one another as we gently squeeze hands. Flan would have been so proud to know that Skeet has lived a good, long life, and if the good doctor were able to brag about that fact, he would do so...right from the grave. That would be all right with us. After all, he was Doctor Flanders Trumbull.

"Until we meet again, my friend," Skeet whispers to Flan, much like he does every year.

The two of us turn, as we have so many times before, and walk hopefully into our future with the same enduring love that has braced us all our lives...this, the treasure we harbor most tenderly within our hearts, the only certainty we have ever known.

"Ah, the two of you look to be in fine feather," William says with a broad smile as we get back into the car. "Where to next?"

"Home," Skeet and I both agree, the word itself a comfort to us both.

And so it goes. On the ride back, we reflect upon our good fortune, Skeet and I, as we hold hands in the backseat of the car. We roll down the windows and feel the fresh air on our faces while reveling in each other's company once more. We make our plans and discuss our dreams. We laugh again... and kiss again. We are together bound through all eternity, our love an endless enchantment, our life forever magical...like the whisper through the trees on a breezy day, or the colorful wildflowers in a vast green meadow, or the warm summer evenings...when everything is still...except for the fireflies at nightfall.

Robin Cannon received her BA and MS degrees from Fordham University in New York City and her Sixth Year Degree in Education Administration from Southern CT State University in New Haven, CT. She has been a schoolteacher for thirty-one years. Robin lives with her husband Bob, daughters Haley and Molly, and son Colin. *Fireflies at Nightfall* is her third book published by **Goose River Press** and is also the third and final installment in the *Tilly Fig* trilogy.